POP and PETER POTTS

Clifford B. Hicks

POP and PETER POTTS

illustrated by Jim Spence

Holt, Rinehart and Winston
New York

Library of Congress Cataloging in Publication Data
Hicks, Clifford B.
    Pop and Peter Potts.
    Summary: A young boy describes his life with his
grandfather who devotes his time to such hobbies as
lion taming, hypnotizing chickens, and inventing the
Great Stone Man.
    [1. Hobbies—Fiction. 2. Grandfathers—Fiction.
3. Humorous stories] I. Spence, Jim, ill. II. Title.
PZ7.H5316Po 1984   [Fic]   84-4526
ISBN 0-03-069627-5

First Edition

Printed in the United States of America
10 9 8 7 6 5 4 3 2 1

ISBN 0-03-069627-5

For Jim and Virginia—
with a special kind of love

Contents

Part III / POP POTTS, HYPNOTIST

...Part I

The Lion That Fell in Love

Waiting for the Time Bomb

Things seldom turn out the way they are supposed to. You might want to remember that.

That's especially true around Pop. Wait and you'll see what I mean. This book is about Pop and his hobbies.

It's also about my sister, Betts. It's about Mike Summers, who can tell coon tracks from possum tracks and is married to Betts. It's also about Willy Peters, who has his hand in everyone else's pocket.

Mainly, though, this book is about Pop and his hobbies. About the lion he tamed, the Great Stone Man he invented, and the chickens he hypnotized.

Living with Pop is like waiting for a time bomb to go off. Every new hobby lights the fuse. You might want to remember that.

Pop started hobbying right after Grandma died, four years ago. Pop isn't really my father. He's my grandfather, but everybody in Fairfield calls him Pop, so I do too.

My sister, Betts, and I came to live with Pop and

3

Grandma right after our folks died in an automobile accident seven years ago. I was six and Betts was thirteen. Three years later, Grandma died of pneumonia, so that left only Pop and Betts and me.

We live in Pop's old farmhouse on the edge of Fairfield. Fairfield, I know for a fact, is the best town in the whole world. Our farm is kind of run-down now. The barn exploded one night while Pop was hobbying with secret formulas. He doesn't farm much anymore; says he can make more money doing odd-job carpentry around Fairfield.

My sister, Betts, raises chickens and sells women's clothing part-time at McClennan's Department Store. She doesn't raise the chickens at McClennan's. Just sells clothes. She married Mike Summers a year ago. I got pretty mad at her for doing that, but Mike turned out better than could be expected. They rented a place a mile up the road. After that Pop took up French cooking as a hobby, but his crêpes and truffles never were eatable, so Betts and Mike moved back in with us a few months later. The grub's a lot better now.

Mike has a job as county agent. I have a paper route and dig up odd jobs whenever I can. We make out, but maybe not as good as some.

Anyway, after Grandma died Pop just moped around the house for months. There was kind of a curtain across his eyes. Then one bright spring day the curtain seemed to vanish. Pop picked up a magazine and started reading it. Within ten minutes he had clipped a coupon from the

4

magazine, filled it out, and sent it off. He announced that he was going to raise giant African earthworms for fun and profit. When those worms arrived they were bigger than garter snakes. Pop never sold a one of them. People were too scared.

After he turned loose the earthworms he became Mysterious Zombie, the World's Greatest Magician. After that he took up weight lifting so he could become the World's Most Perfectly Developed Man. Pop normally is as skinny as a whittled toothpick, and those weights peeled ten pounds off his already-bare bones.

Now he was saying something about a lion! He was on the phone in the kitchen, his voice as high as a kite, the way it gets when he's excited.

"Noon train?" he was shouting. Pop always shouts into the phone. "You're sure that lion will be on the noon freight tomorrow?"

It made me a little nervous, until I figured I hadn't heard right. I should have known better.

"No!" he shouted over the phone. "Don't you worry about the cage for the lion. My check will cover it too."

He hung up and came walking into the parlor, eyes snapping out of the wrinkles that cut every which way across his long face.

"Holy smokes," he mumbled under his breath. "I'll be plegged if I don't own a real live lion!" He sat down on the sofa, his short legs barely reaching the floor.

"Pop, what are you talking about?" Already I had a feeling.

5

He slapped his overalls. "Pete, you're looking at a real live lion tamer. I bought me a lion, and, by jabbers, I'll tame him!"

I jumped off the chair. "You mean you've got a lion coming here?"

"Yep. A real live honest-to-goodness lion."

"I'm moving out!"

"No you aren't. You're going to help me tame him, Pete."

"I'm moving out," I said again, knowing I didn't mean it, and, anyway, it wouldn't change Pop's mind.

The last time I moved out was Fourth of July, and I didn't exactly move out, I just tried to run away from Fairfield. Maybe you'd like to hear about that before you hear any more about the lion. Joey Gootz and I had planned a big Fourth of July celebration, and it turned out even bigger than we figured.

On the Fourth, everybody in Fairfield comes downtown for the big parade. After the parade, the mayor makes a long speech that nobody listens to. Then, after one minute of silent prayer, the American Legion loads some powder into the old cannon on the town square. They light the fuse, and the cannon makes a bang you can hear pretty near a mile away.

Anyway, Joey and I figured we'd make a little extra excitement that year. The night before the Fourth we filled a tin can with cement. As soon as it hardened, we snuck down to the town square and slipped the can down the muzzle of the cannon. It fit just as nice as you please.

6

The next day, after the parade, there must have been two thousand people gathered around that old cannon. The mayor gave his speech. He always gives the same one. I've forgotten what it's about.

Well, when he got through talking there was a minute of silence. Then the honor guard from the American Legion marched up to the back of the cannon. They shoved in a bag of black powder—Joey said afterward it was bigger than usual—put in a fuse, and closed up the back door. Then they touched a match to the fuse.

I guess Joey knew that something was going wrong, because he started to run while the fuse was still burning. I couldn't get my legs in motion.

Blam!

The old cannon bucked about two feet in the air, and when it came down, the muzzle looked like a peeled banana. The tin can full of cement came sailing out like a catcher's throw to second base. You could see it plain as day. It arched up toward the sky and soared for about two blocks.

Does your town have a steel water tank? Ours does now. That's what Joey and I hadn't figured on. The cannon was aimed smack at Fairfield's old wooden tank.

The tin can hit that tank near the bottom. You could see the boards fly apart all the way from the town square.

The water squirted out of the hole like it was coming from a giant water pistol. It shot clear across Main

7

Street and hit Mrs. Smithers's prize rose garden like a bomb. Mrs. Smithers has been touchy about those roses ever since they won first prize at the county fair three years ago.

I'm telling you, it was like holding a bouquet under Niagara Falls. The rose bushes vanished—poof!—in the first blast of water. They needed weeding anyway.

Joey and I got all the way out to Highway 16 before Pop found us. He never did ask us whether we knew anything about that can full of cement in the cannon. I think he was afraid of our answer. To this day nobody in Fairfield knows who did it, but I think Mrs. Smithers suspects Joey and me. Mrs. Smithers is always very suspicious of us.

I have a pretty big conscience for such a short, skinny kid, and I've wanted to get the water tank off my chest for months. I always say that if you can't live with yourself, nobody else can live with you, either. You might want to remember that; it makes a good thought for the day.

Anyway, that was the last time I wanted to run away from home, until Pop told me about the lion. Then I was tempted to hit the road again.

He talked to me awhile, trying to persuade me that lion taming would be an exciting new hobby. Finally I asked him where he got the lion.

"A zoo in Chicago. They had too many of them."

"How are you aiming to tame it?"

"Galloping gelatin, Pete, do you think I'd order a lion without knowing exactly how to tame the beast?

8

Just last Sunday I read a magazine article about a lion tamer. It's simple. All you need is a whip and an old chair and—" He jumped to his feet. "Pete, we have work to do! We have to build a cage for Prince!"

You see how Pop is? Already he'd named that lion.

The fence around the old pigpen was still solid. Pop decided it would make a good cage for a lion. I helped him spike the old barn beams to the posts, building up a set of heavy poles a good fifteen feet high.

In the evening, Betts pitched in, too. She knows even better than I do that there's no arguing with Pop when he takes on a new hobby. Around the poles we ran three layers of fencing and topped that off with some barbed wire. By the time we reinforced the old gate, Betts said the cage looked strong enough to hold an elephant.

Before I go any further I'd better tell you something about Mike and Betts—and myself, too.

I'm not very good-looking. I have a wad of freckles, and hair that stands out every which way. My looks never worried me much until I was seven. That's when I got a secret passion in Sunday School for Minnie Wumpser. Minnie could say the books of the Bible forward and then backward without taking more than three breaths. Every year, on the Christmas program, she'd stand up in front of the whole church and reel off those names in both directions.

Minnie doesn't really have much to do with my sister, Betts, but maybe you'd like to hear more about her. I was in love with Minnie in those days. That's

9

another reason I'm writing this book. I want to get all of these deep secrets off my chest, secrets I've never told anyone. Whenever Minnie gets nervous she runs her nose across the sleeve of her dress. I think it's kind of cute.

This one year, during the Christmas program, Minnie got up as usual to recite the books of the Bible. As soon as she looked out at the crowd, she ran her nose along her sleeve. She let out the biggest sneeze I ever heard. That made her more nervous, so she rubbed her nose again. She started sneezing like bloody murder. Joey told me later that when her back had been turned he'd shaken some red pepper across her sleeve because she got a better report card than he did.

Minnie's eyes were running, and she staggered blindly off to the side of the platform, where Bobby Schultz was waiting to show off his performing dog. There was a sudden yelp as Minnie stepped on Bobby Schultz's dog's tail.

The dog was kind of a yellow color, and I swear all you could see was a yellow streak as he took off up the aisle. He was running so fast he didn't even see the Christmas tree. It came down with a crash, and ornaments and lights were flying every which way. I guess the broken lights caused a short circuit and blew a fuse, because every light in the church went off.

Down in the basement some of the ladies were fixing supper for everybody. We have a big electric stove in our church, and of course it went out, too. There weren't any extra fuses that year. Did you ever eat cold macaroni and cheese?

I don't remember how Minnie crept into this book, but I'm glad she did. When I started writing it I promised myself I'd be perfectly honest and tell everything just the way I see it, so I can't hide how I feel about Minnie. I always say you've got to be honest with yourself or you won't be honest with anybody else. You might want to remember that; it makes a good thought for the day.

I'd better get back to Mike and Betts. Betts is the best-looking girl in the county. Mike says so, and I agree, with one possible exception. Betts and I aren't like most brothers and sisters who argue all the time. Maybe that's because she's felt responsible for me ever since the folks died. Besides, she can swat a softball farther than anyone else in the girls' league. I get along fine with Betts.

I get along fine with Mike too. We have a Secret Place (that's what we call it) out in Kellogg's woods. It's right on the edge of a marsh, and if you go there real quiet early in the morning you can watch muskrat and mink and even a family of red fox doing what each of them is supposed to do. Mike is like a big brother who knows just about everything.

...2

How Prince Joined the Family

The next morning while Mike was at work, Betts, Pop, and I climbed into Pop's truck and headed toward the railroad station to pick up the lion. We arrived just as the noon freight train rolled in. Sure enough, there was a big cage aboard, only it was all covered over with canvas so you couldn't see what was inside.

Willy Peters was standing on the platform, his sharp eyes taking in everything as usual. Willy loafs his way through life, but a lot of money seems to drift from other folks's pockets into his. Pop persuaded Willy to take off his fancy coat and help us slide the cage from the freight car onto the truck.

"That dog sure must be a whopper," Willy said, listening to the shuffling sounds inside the cage.

Somehow I was glad Pop didn't correct him. Betts and I were getting kind of excited about that lion ourselves, and we didn't want anyone else to see Prince until we did.

Back home, Pop drove up beside the pigpen. He was

13

so excited he couldn't talk. We managed to slide the cage down some old planks, wiggling it until one end of the cage rested just inside the gate.

Pop reached through the fence and untied a piece of the canvas. He was mighty careful not to get his hands in the way when he pulled open the door of the cage. From behind the cage we couldn't see a thing, and for two or three minutes we stood there waiting.

"Crowbait!" Pop muttered.

He poked a stick through an air hole in the canvas and pried loose a growl. I was pretty scared.

That lion didn't leap out. He just walked slowly into the pen and sat there, stretching and yawning. As soon as I saw him I snorted, and there was a giggle from Betts.

Prince was the sorriest, skinniest, ugliest lion I ever did see. He had a great big face covered with wrinkles, kind of like Pop's. His mouth turned up at the corners, as though he was grinning. A wad of scraggly black hair framed his face. No kidding, he sat there *smiling*. There were big spots eaten out of his hide, and when he yawned you could see that some of his teeth were missing.

"Hi, Prince!" said Pop, his voice trembling with excitement. Prince strolled over to the side of the cage and rubbed up against the fence where Pop had been resting one knee. He purred, and it sounded like thunder. Pop started to reach a hand through the fence.

"Careful, Pop!" warned Betts.

Pop's shaking hand paused a moment, but then

14

moved slow and easy through the fence, touching an ear. Prince raised his head so Pop's fingers could rest on his mane. Pop started scratching, and the lion shook loose a purr that sounded like a freight train a mile away.

"See!" said Pop, his voice shaking in triumph. "You have to make friends with the lion first. See how easy it is to be a lion tamer?"

Prince swung his big head around and looked at Betts for the first time. His eyes melted into the wrinkles of his face, and he padded over to Betts's feet. I've heard of love at first sight, and this was it.

Betts smiled down at him. When she reached both arms through the fence and put them around his neck, he rolled over at her feet.

Pop ran to the house while Betts and Prince made purring noises at each other. When he came back he was carrying an old snake whip, his rifle, and a kitchen chair.

"You're not going to try anything today, are you Pop?" I asked.

"You're durn right I am!" he said. "You have to show a lion who's boss right off the bat." He handed me the rifle. "Now if I get into any trouble, don't aim at Prince. Just raise a cloud of dust in front of his nose while I slip out of the way."

When he unlatched the gate I noticed his hands were shaking. I didn't figure that was a very good sign. He slipped into the cage, slamming the gate shut behind him.

16

"Here, Prince!" he called softly.

Prince looked once in his direction, then gazed up at Betts again.

Pop took a couple of steps toward him, holding the chair in one hand and the whip in the other. "Here, Prince!"

Betts edged over toward me. The lion watched her go, then rolled to his feet, yawning. He walked over to Pop, standing there with his nose inches from the chair. Pop barely touched him on the nose, and Prince backed away, still purring.

Pop was getting mad. He cracked the whip once, but Prince didn't flick a hair, so Pop lowered the chair a little.

"Stick him with the clothes pole," he hollered.

"No," I said, "I'm hanging on to this rifle."

Betts got the clothes pole and stuck it through the fence, touching Prince on the behind. When he looked around and saw it was Betts, he melted at her feet again.

Pop set the chair on the ground and lowered the whip. Finally he walked over to Prince and slowly reached out his hand. He tickled the lion on the belly.

Within four or five minutes Pop was sitting in the dust beside Prince, scratching him behind the ears. That lion didn't want to be tamed: he was already so friendly he wouldn't hurt a flea on his own flea-bitten hide.

"You slab-footed, slat-bellied, snaggle-haired beast, you!" Pop muttered, but there was love in his voice.

17

"There was nothing in that magazine article about taming a lion like you."

Before the week was out the four of us—Pop, Betts, Mike, and myself—were romping around inside the cage with Prince every minute we could spare.

Most of all Prince liked Betts. Every time she came around the cage he'd get a cow look on his face and roll his eyes at her.

Though lion taming wasn't the dangerous hobby Pop had expected, he was having fun. He built some small platforms and bolted them to the cage posts so they formed steps up around the inside of the cage, like the spiral steps inside the dome of the state capitol. When the steps were finished he jumped up on the lowest one and sat there a minute, then jumped down again. Right away Prince got the idea and jumped up onto the platform.

I'm not kidding, within fifteen or twenty minutes Pop taught Prince to leap from platform to platform all around the cage. It was quite a sight to see the two of them racing each other up and down the steps.

With Pop's help, Prince learned to walk on his hind legs too. He'd walk all around the cage, with his tail waggling through the dust.

Naturally the word about Prince got around Fairfield pretty fast. All the kids came flocking out to see the lion. I'm telling you, I was a real hero. Grown-ups followed the kids. They pretty near jumped out of their

18

skins when they saw Pop and Betts and me playing with a lion.

During the day Pop never let Prince out of the cage. He said it might make the people of Fairfield a little nervous, but I couldn't see why. That lion wouldn't hurt a mouse. After dark, though, Pop would unlatch the gate and Prince would come trotting into the house at his heels. Prince sat by the easy chair while Pop read the paper.

Late one afternoon, after I got back from mowing Mrs. Dills's lawn, I headed for the pigpen to play with Prince. As I rounded the corner of the house I saw Betts dancing around the cage, whooping and laughing until the tears rolled.

"Look at them!" she gasped.

When I glanced at the cage, I just about jumped through my baseball cap. There was Prince, standing on his hind legs like a man, my old baby chair gripped in his mouth and a tiny whip tied to his right front paw. We got the whip at the county fair last year.

But it was Pop that doubled me up. He was crouched on one of the platforms by the fence, glaring at Prince. His lips were curled back to show his one gold tooth, and deep snarls were coming up through his throat. Every time Prince waved the whip, Pop rocked forward on the platform as though he was going to leap.

By sundown, when Mike arrived home, Pop and Prince had worked out a regular act. Prince would

19

stand on his hind legs in the center of the pen while Pop crouched in the canvas-covered entry box—the same crate Prince had been shipped in. Then, when Prince waved the whip, Pop would come slinking out on his hands and feet, snarling and waving his head.

Prince would start moving in on him. Rearing back and growling, Pop followed the whip from platform to platform.

They had a fine ending to the act. Prince would edge up, like he was scared, and stick his nose into Pop's snarling mouth.

It wasn't long until everybody in Fairfield was dropping around again, late in the afternoon, to watch the new act. Old Man Simpson laughed so hard he threw his spine out of joint. He had to spend two weeks in the hospital at Middle City.

You've got to give Willy Peters credit. Willy's as sharp as anybody I've ever seen. It was Willy who cornered me in front of the movie the next Saturday afternoon.

"Why don't you make some money off that dog-eared lion, Pete?" he asked.

"He's just a pet," I said. "How are we going to make any money off him?"

"Do you figure Pop would split one-third with me on anything we make?"

"Sure," I said, knowing Pop couldn't lose on a deal like that.

"I'll be out tomorrow to see your grandfather."

21

...3

How We Made a Wad of Money in Show Business

The next Saturday Willy Peters showed up at the house. Naturally it was just about time to eat. Betts and I were fixing chicken pie, the kind with lots of gravy inside, hidden by a thin crust that sort of melts into nothing when it hits your mouth.

All through the meal, Pop and Willy shouted at each other. Betts kept winking at me and smiling at their talk.

Finally Pop said, "All right, Willy. You'll get your fifty-two percent, but, by jabbers, you'll do some work for it!"

That very afternoon Jethro Plotkin from the lumberyard showed up with a lot of boards. He built some seats all around Prince's cage. Also he built a covered entry box, with one door inside the cage and the other outside.

Late in the afternoon Willy showed up with a lot of old army tents. He told Jethro to rip them into big

23

pieces. Then he and Jethro rigged the pieces so the canvas covered the cage but would fall to the ground when Willy pulled a rope. It was just like pulling the curtain on a stage.

Willy wasn't parting with a penny, though. When Jethro left late that evening it was Pop who paid him off, not Willy.

The next afternoon Pop told me to hop in the pickup truck and take a ride with him, there was something he wanted to see. A few miles down Highway 16 we began seeing the signs.

STOP AT FAIRFIELD—SEE THE LION WHO TAMES A MAN
WILLY PETERS ENTERPRISES

Naturally Willy had his name in capital letters. Down the road a holler was another sign:

STOP AT FAIRFIELD—SEE THE ONLY LION TAMER WHO
GIVES HIS WHIP TO THE LION
WILLY PETERS ENTERPRISES

The next morning I went over to Mr. Snyder's farm to pick some tomatoes. When I got back to the house, there were a few out-of-state cars parked on the front lawn. Behind the house, Betts was selling tickets, wearing a summer dress instead of her jeans. She had her hair all fixed up, too. I'm not much to make a fuss over women, but she looked so pretty I was proud she was my sister.

Sitting on the bleachers were thirty-five or forty peo-

24

ple, roaring at the sight of Prince taming Pop. Prince had the whip tied to his right front paw and was rearing back on his hind legs. Pop was snarling down at him from the top platform.

Willy winked at Mike and me. Even though it was the hottest day of summer Willy was dressed in a bright red vest, and over his arm he carried a yellow cane. "Not bad," he said. "Not bad, at a dollar apiece."

Well, I'm telling you, within two weeks the money was rolling in so fast we didn't have time to spend it. Pop paid four hundred dollars on the mortgage, and Betts bought a couple of new dresses she'd been wanting. We even started a special savings account for Prince in the First National Bank, to buy him horsemeat in his old age.

Willy sent a photograph to every newspaper in the state. It showed Pop snarling down from one of the platforms at Prince, who was rigged out like a lion tamer, whip in his paw, chair in his mouth, and a pistol belt around his belly. It was a picture that would stop anybody's eye, all right, and every one of the newspapers used it. Then both *Time* and *Newsweek* carried articles about Pop and Prince, and people started driving in by the thousands.

We'd pack three or four hundred people in for a performance at a dollar a whack, five or six hundred on weekends. Pop and Prince were bigshots now, practicing by lantern light two or three nights a week, changing and polishing their act. Finally they built up a

25

performance that lasted almost an hour. It ended with Prince cracking the whip while Pop jumped through a flaming hoop.

That's the way things went most of the summer. Pop could get credit in any store in town now. So much tourist business had come to Fairfield that Marty Simms, who owns the drugstore and is president of the chamber of commerce, was talking about moving the city limits out beyond our place and running Pop for mayor.

It was about then, though, that I noticed a change coming over Pop. He was getting kind of listless. He didn't really show much interest in the performance. He was snappish, too, and would snarl at the supper table if his steak wasn't cooked just right.

One night, while Willy Peters was there, he went storming out of the house, leaving the rest of us to worry over him. Betts said she thought he was sick and maybe we should call a doctor.

"Get Doc Hemphill," suggested Willy with a grin. Doc Hemphill is the county veterinarian.

When Pop came back, Betts told him what Willy had said, figuring it might get a laugh. It made Pop madder than a mud hen.

Pop started ranting at everybody. "By jabbers, nobody appreciates me around here. I've got to get me something to occupy my mind."

He started fingering his shirttail then, and in a few minutes he was ripping it. All of a sudden he jumped up out of his chair and started for the bedroom. In the

26

doorway he met Prince. Pop gave the lion a shove against the doorframe that rocked the house.

"Keep that beast out of here!" he bellowed.

Prince never came in the house again.

I knew from the ripped shirttail what was happening. Pop was tired of his old hobby and wanted to start a new one.

Sure enough, the next day he bought a book on poultry breeding and announced he was going to cross a parrot with a rooster and get a creature that would shout "Get up!" in the morning.

That afternoon Pop lay in bed reading the book and pretending he was sick. He wouldn't even listen when Willy and I tried to talk him into his performance.

"Blue bottles! A man can be sick if he's sick. Pete, you'll have to do the act. I'd ask Mike to do it, but he has his own job to handle."

I'd seen Pop and Prince do the act a good many times, but I wasn't very sure of myself. Besides, I didn't want to imitate a lion.

"You've *got* to do it, Pete," said Willy. "The money's rolling in by the bucketful. We can't stop now."

Well, feeling like a darn fool, I finally ran across that cage on all fours in front of three hundred people, trying to remember everything that Pop did. Prince helped by waving me on with his whip, showing me which way to go. The crowd seemed pleased as punch, but I knew my performance didn't come up to Pop's. When I tried to snarl, it came out kind of high-pitched, like a giggle.

27

Next day, Saturday, Pop said he was sick again, and we all knew then that I'd be doing the act every day.

That evening Mike was giving a talk about raccoons to the Boy Scouts. Betts and I drifted down to the cage about sunset and heaved Prince his dinner. Standing by the cage, Betts started talking about Mike and how happy they were. Almost made me want to get married, too. The setting sun was shining on her face, and there was a softness in her eyes. I felt very close to her just then and put my arm around her.

Betts leaned over and kissed me on the forehead.

Right then, from the cage at our feet, came a rumble that grew into a roar. Then the heavy fence began heaving. Betts swung around with a flip of her hair. I glanced around, too, and saw Prince ripping his claws down the fence. His head was weaving back and forth, and his hind legs were gathered under him like springs.

"Why, he's jealous, Pete!" said Betts. "Imagine! Poor Prince, don't you understand? Pete and I are brother and sister. Sure we like each other. We grew up together. But you're something special, Prince."

I know she didn't mean it the way it sounded.

She purred at Prince through the fence for two or three minutes, and he finally calmed down. When we turned toward the house, though, and she put her hand on my arm, there was another snarl behind us.

The next day, Sunday, was a beauty. Willy showed up about noon.

"The biggest Sunday crowd of the season, I reckon,"

28

he said, looking at me with a dollar sign in his eye. "And a special day too."

"Why special?" I asked.

"Well, day before yesterday, Pete, I airmailed some pictures of you and Prince to a movie studio. I named you Nature Boy. This morning I got a phone call that there'll be a movie man out to look you over this afternoon. Promise to let me do the talking, and you'll be in the movies."

"I don't especially want to be in the movies," I said.

"Think of the money, Pete. And the fame. Why, every girl in the country will be wild about you."

"All right," I said. "I'll be in the movies."

"Good! Here's the pitch, Pete. I've got the American Legion band coming out today to give the show some snap. Don't comb your hair this afternoon. Just let it shoot out all over your head like Nature Boy. At the end of the act, get fiercer and fiercer. Then leap at Prince's throat and start wrestling him as though you really mean it. The band will give you a big blast to end the show."

Willy paused, looking down at his feet. "Pete, if that movie contract comes through, we'll split the money. I wouldn't give you half if I didn't like you so well."

By the middle of the afternoon the cars were packed solid all over our place and overflowing into Oostermeyer's oat field across the road. That was all right. We'd already paid double for the oats.

I'd like to forget that afternoon, though.

29

...4

How Prince Put Willy Peters out of Business

The American Legion band came out in the school bus and put on a smart marching exhibition before our act.

The canvas was in place around the cage. I could hear Willy inside, talking to Prince while he strapped on the toy whip. I slipped through the outside door of the covered entry box and latched it behind me. Inside the dark box it was as lonesome as a graveyard at midnight.

The band started blaring away, and I heard Willy slip out of the cage. When there was a loud murmur from the crowd, I knew Mike had jerked the rope that let down the canvas. Those tourists were getting their first peek at Prince. I mussed up my hair like Willy said, and slipped the door in front of me to one side so I could hunch out into the pen.

31

Prince stood there proudly on his hind legs, belly sleek from our feed, eyes sparkling at the crowd, whiskers standing out stiff around his mouth. He looked like he was straight out of the jungle, and he moved slow and easy, as though he had plenty of time.

What stopped me in my tracks was the sight of Prince's tail. Instead of licking back and forth in the dirt the way it usually did, it followed him like a poker, stiff and motionless. It sort of hypnotized me. Then he started waving the whip, and I knew it was time to slink into the cage.

The band was playing a march, but I hardly heard it. I had an urge to slam the door in front of me and just sit inside that box forever. All of a sudden I knew I was scared. My head and shoulders started trembling. Maybe that's what shook some sense into me. It was the same old Prince, same old act. Nothing to be scared of. I started to move.

As I crawled out of the box my hair fell down across my eyes, bothering me, and I stuck out my lower lip and blew it out of the way. Prince was edging closer now, and from the look in his eyes I knew something was wrong.

Just once he snarled, but the sound came straight from the jungle. I jumped like a rabbit in the middle of a plowed field.

Looking back on it, I can see where I made my big mistake. Instead of loping on all fours like Pop always did, I ran for my life around the edge of the cage.

32

Behind me came a growl that sounded like thunder. I leaped up on the lowest platform, glancing back over my shoulder. I'm telling you, that sight would have frozen Tarzan in his tracks. Prince had edged in between me and the entry box. He'd dropped the chair out of his mouth and was whirling around in the dust, trying to claw the whip from his paw. If animals can cuss, there were some mighty bad words rumbling up through his throat, words that scared my hair to attention.

I never moved so fast in my life. I just kept right on jumping from platform to platform, though I knew Prince could follow me. By now the band had stopped playing and there was scarcely a sound from the crowd. Somewhere in the distance I heard a shrill scream from Marty Simms's little girl, then a quiet that stretched from here to heaven.

From the highest platform I tried to climb right on over the top of the fence, but my shirt got tangled in the strands of barbed wire. I looked down just in time to see Prince free his paw. Then he was running, smooth and cold as a killer, toward the lowest platform. One jump carried him six feet through the air, and he landed on the step without a sound.

Turning his face toward me, he opened up with a roar that shook the cage. I could practically read his mind. Betts was *his* girl, those eyes said, and anybody she loved was his worst enemy.

For a long minute he stood there, whiskers bristling,

33

watching me try to claw the barbed wire loose. Then he leaped for the next platform.

There were seven steps up, and he stopped on each one. We both knew he could reach me in a split second even if I got myself loose. By now all the men were hollering and the women were screaming.

When he got to the fourth platform I guess I was so scared I didn't hear the click of the gate. But I did hear the voice, and so did Prince. Did you ever hear a real quiet sound in the middle of an uproar? So quiet it seems louder than all the other noises put together? That's the way it was with Betts's voice. She was standing in the middle of the cage, calling softly to Prince.

"Betts!" I hollered. "Betts! Get out of the cage!"

But she kept on talking, not words exactly, just purring sounds that came up through her throat and reached out to tame that beast. His ears had been laying flat against his head, but now they picked up a little.

The more she purred, the quieter her voice sounded until you could just barely hear it. All of a sudden Prince looked up at me and turned loose the thunder again, but there wasn't a pause in the sounds from Betts's lips.

I was watching Prince's tail. When it began twitching just a little I turned quick and went back to work on the barbed wire. I kept praying I would have enough time to get out of the cage and get Pop's rifle

34

before Betts was killed. Somehow I managed to climb out of my shirt. I reckon there was a little of the jungle in me too, as I moved like a monkey up the barbed wire. As I pivoted across the top I saw Mike running for the house to get Pop's rifle. I hit the ground with a jolt that shook me almost senseless.

It was just as I staggered to my feet that Prince leaped. He hit the ground without a sound and stalked slowly across the cage toward Betts. She didn't back up, and I guess she was wise. Except for the soft purr from her lips there wasn't a sound, as Prince slipped toward her, slow and easy as Satan. When he finally reached her he crouched down, coiled like a spring.

Her hand moved down slow and touched him on his favorite tickle spot behind the right ear. His body twitched. Then she was scratching his thick mane, and he folded up at her feet. For two or three minutes she purred in his ear, then turned and walked across the cage to the gate.

Willy Peters was standing by, his face as white as my Sunday shirt. He slammed the gate behind her. Then Betts had her arms around me, and I guess I had mine around her, too. It's a good thing she was my sister, in front of all those people.

"Pete!" she said. "Oh, Pete! It was just like I was caught up there on that fence, too."

Just about then Prince shook loose a roar that could be heard clear over on County Road. When he saw Betts with her arms around me he hit the side of

36

the cage like an elephant. Then he started streaking around the fence. He spotted the platforms and ran up them with a roar. At the top step he tried to leap over the barbed wire, but he couldn't get a good jump and fell back into the dust.

There's not much more to tell about Pop's lion taming. He's looking around for a new hobby. Betts and Mike are still starry-eyed over each other. I guess being married isn't so bad after all. For every bad there's a good hidden somewhere. You might want to remember that; it makes a good thought for the day.

Within a week of my narrow escape, Willy Peters started getting friendly with the eighteen-year-old Oostermeyer boy, who shot up to seven feet two inches tall this year. Willy couldn't decide whether to organize a professional basketball team or wait and see if Benny Oostermeyer would keep on growing to circus size. He waited just a little too long. Benny got a job painting ceilings for Gurney Phelps.

And Prince? Well, he's back at the zoo in Chicago. The zoo man hopped a plane as soon as he read about what happened. The only reason he'd sold Prince in the first place was because Prince was too friendly— acted more like a dog than a lion. He offered to buy Prince back at the same price, but Pop held out for twice as much and got it.

The other day we got a letter from the zoo man. He

said Prince is the best animal in the whole zoo these days. He roars and shows his claws every minute he's awake. The letter said Prince might be in love. He's rubbing noses with the lioness in the cage next door.

Betts seemed unhappy when she heard about the lioness. You figure women. I can't.

...Part II

Pop and the Great Stone Man

...5

How Pop Found a New Hobby

When Pop found out it was impossible to cross a parrot with a rooster, he dropped poultry breeding like it was a handful of fried BBs. He began sending out coupons by the fistful.

About ten days after he sent out the first batch, the results began showing up in the mailbox. First came a booklet on making jams and jellies, then an advertisement for a course in carving totem poles. There was a book on playing tunes by bonking yourself on the head with your mouth open, and instructions for hunting anteaters in Africa.

There was a course to learn the Spanish language: "Study Fifteen Minutes a Day," it said, "and Speak Spanish in One Month!" Pop never learned much Spanish, but our mailbox has been labeled Señor Potts ever since.

Then there was the taxidermy course: "Mount Birds and Animals in Lifelike Poses." A week after the booklet arrived, Pop shot an old crow in the south pasture. That crow is now mounted on the south wall of our

41

living room. It has one glass eye that follows you wherever you go. The other one stares at the ceiling.

Then, out of the blue, Pop settled down on his new hobby like a pigeon coming home to roost. He was sitting in his easy chair and let out his breath in a long sigh. From that moment he wasn't jumpy but friendly as you please.

"What's your new hobby?" I asked him, after he had sat there, relaxed and daydreaming, for half an hour.

He was startled. "How'd you know I had a new hobby?"

"It's not hard to tell. For one thing, you quit ripping your shirttail. What's the hobby?"

"I'm not saying a word, Pete, until I try it. In the mail today was a catalog telling all about it. I'm ordering some materials special delivery. As soon as they come, I'll give the hobby a try." Just talking about it, he began to get excited. "This is the best one of all, Pete. This one will make me famous."

He was right, too. It *did* make him famous.

About a week later a box came special delivery, a box so heavy it took two men to carry it into the house. Pop was at work at the time, and I had a notion to pry open the lid just to take a peek, but finally decided I'd do better not to risk it.

When Pop came home from work and saw the box, his eyes lit up like airplane beacons. He could hardly wait to tear it open. That night was a good night for it, as Betts and Mike were eating supper in town. Pop

42

wouldn't have to explain his hobby to anybody until he'd tried it.

There was no way to get rid of me, though. While he got a crowbar and started prying open the box, I got out some strawberry Jell-O to tide me over until we ate supper.

"Look here, Pete," he said, when the lid finally came off.

Inside the box was the strangest boxful I've ever seen. What it was was a big rock. Just a big rock and nothing else, except a little package with three pointy chisels inside.

"What's the rock for?" I asked.

"I'm a sculptor, Pete. In fact, I'll probably be one of the greatest sculptors in the history of the world. I'll make statues. Beautiful statues that go in art museums, and places like that. I'll make statues like all those famous ones."

"What famous statues?"

"Well, statues like . . . like . . ." Finally he paused and looked at the instruction book. "Like the beautiful Venus de Milo. Pete, beauty is what makes the world a fitter place to live in."

"Oh." That's probably a good thought for the day.

I never knew a rock could be so heavy. It took both of us to lift it out of the box and heave it up onto the dining-room table. Pop told me to get a hammer from the tool shed while he looked over the instruction book.

Within ten minutes chips of stone were flying around the room. I felt like I was under bombardment. I ducked this way and that, until finally I gave up and crawled under the table at Pop's feet.

Curiosity got the better of me. "What are you sculpting?" I hollered.

Whap! *Whap*! The hammer hit the chisel two strong blows. "I'm making a Greek lady with her dress down around her hips."

Suddenly his head appeared upside down beneath the rim of the table. "Hey, Pete! Get up here and pose for me."

There's no arguing with Pop. I found myself in the middle of the living room, my face turned to one side and one hand on my hip. Pop had taken down the living-room curtain and draped it around my hips. That worried me, because anybody who was driving by could see me right through the window. Including Minnie Wumpser, except that Minnie doesn't drive yet.

Pop took time out for a bite of Jell-O. There was a loud crunch, and he grabbed for his mouth. Out came a jagged chip of stone. Pop looked at it foolishly then heaved it into the corner behind the floor lamp.

I was surprised when I looked at that big rock for the first time. No question about it, all that chipping had done something to it. Sure enough, it looked a little bit like a human figure. I had to admit it. To tell the truth, though, it looked more like Fats Simpkins with his pants around his knees than a Greek goddess.

44

The stomach drooped out in front, and one arm looked longer than the other. Fats has the stomach problem, but not the long arm.

Pop stood there, hammer and chisel in hand, eyes shining, waiting for me to speak. Finally he couldn't hold out any longer. "What do you think?"

I kept him in suspense for a full minute. Then: "It looks fine for your first try, Pop." I was anxious to keep him interested in a hobby.

"I still have a lot of work to do on this statue. Her left knee doesn't look quite right. And I've either got to lengthen one arm or shorten the other. Maybe when I finish this sculpture I'll enter it in the contest at the state art museum. Probably will win first prize." The air came sucking through his teeth. "Maybe I better wait though, and try another statue or two. I might sculpt one that's even better. What do you think, Pete?"

"Better wait, Pop."

Later that night, as I fell asleep, I could hear him muttering to himself. "Life-size figure," he was saying, and "put a little meat on Pete's bones so he'll look more like a Greek goddess."

...6

How Mike and Pop and I Visited the Quarry at Midnight

I live in a pretty normal house, and things went along pretty normally for a couple of weeks. Pop kept hacking away at rocks he found out behind the henhouse, until the parlor was filled with statues. He made statues of men wrapped in sheets, and ladies without much on, and even some statues that didn't look like anything to me, but he said they were modern art. You could scarcely sit down in the living room for fear of sitting on Venus de Milo.

Then it happened. Pop was sitting at the table sculpting a statue of a horse with a horn early one evening when all of a sudden he threw down his sculpting tools.

Oh-oh, I thought, he's through with this hobby and he'll begin looking around for another one.

I was wrong—dead wrong.

"Pete," he said, looking up at me out of the wrinkles

47

in his face, "I'm through with practicing. Now I'm ready for some *real* sculpting."

"What do you mean, Pop?"

Pop replied as solemn as an owl, "Pete, I'm ready to start sculpting a life-size figure."

Thinking I'd kid him along, I said, "There's that big boulder out by the creek. Can't weigh more than ten or twelve tons. Do you want me to borrow Oostermeyer's tractor and haul the boulder through the side of the house?"

Pop was serious. "No-o-o," he said, considering the idea carefully. "No, that's the wrong kind of stone. But after dark, you and I and Mike are going to pay a visit to the quarry. I reckon we can find a slab of stone down there that'll be just about what I need."

The quarry is four miles down a back road, where they dynamite out the rock, then crush it into gravel. Most of the gravel is sold to the highway department and the ready-mix-concrete factory.

"Why wait until after dark? We won't be able to see what we're doing."

"I'll tell you, Pete. Nobody in Fairfield knows I'm sculpting yet. I aim to keep it that way until I'm ready to spring the big surprise on them. All of a sudden they'll discover they have a world-famous sculptor right on the edge of town." Pop was rubbing his hands together as though he'd already won the biggest prize in the world. "We'll go down there after dark for a slab of stone. Nobody will see my masterpiece until it's finished."

48

Mike came home about dusk wearing his good pants that he wears to work every day. I always say that good pants are pretty near useless in impressing anyone; it's the body in them that counts. That's a good thought for the day.

Pop asked Mike if he'd help us, that it wouldn't take but a few minutes, so Mike didn't even bother to change his clothes. Mike mussed up my hair and said maybe we'd see a deer in the woods down by the quarry. Like I said, Mike knows all about wild things.

Before we climbed into the pickup truck, Pop tossed in some things he figured we'd need. He took along two flashlights, four fence posts, some long timbers, and a block and tackle. Just in case you don't know what a block and tackle is, it's a rope strung around some pulleys. It gives you a lot more lifting power than you'd have otherwise.

The moon was just coming up over the quarry. Off to one side, down by the creek, we could hear the frogs *grumf*ing, and every once in a while there'd be a *swishety-swish* overhead as a bat flew by. There wasn't a soul around that time of night.

We walked down the little road into the quarry. There were big chunks of rock lying all around, blasted loose by the dynamite, like gravestones somebody had toppled over. If I'd been alone, I would have been mighty scared down there. The beams from our flashlights made the shadows dance.

"Here's a good one," I said, pointing to a rock about the size of a bushel basket.

49

Pop just shook his head. He was very particular. A couple of times Mike pointed out some mighty fine-looking rocks, but Pop didn't want them. Finally Mike and I sat down on a slab and talked about how owls and coons see at night. I could tell Mike was jumpy to get back to Betts.

Suddenly Pop called, "I've found it! Here's just the one!"

We climbed over and took a look at the stone. I pretty near passed out when I saw it. That slab of rock was longer than any man I've ever seen and measured about two feet square at the base. It was the biggest piece of rock in the whole quarry.

"Pop," I said, "we'll never be able to lift that slab of stone."

"Yes we will. That's why I brought Mike along. Any young 'un that's married to my granddaughter is probably man enough to help out."

Pop went back and drove the pickup truck down into the quarry. He backed it around until it was close to the stone. For a minute he stood there with the flashlight in his hand, patting the stone as though it was already the finest statue in the world.

Both Mike and I figured Pop was crazy, but we followed his directions. First we laid out a couple of timbers so they formed a ramp from the bed of the pickup truck down to the ground, a few inches from the slab. Then we put a rock close by the slab and put the longest timber over the rock and under the edge of the stone to make a long lever. Mike and Pop got on

50

the other end of the timber while I stood by with a fence post.

"Heave!" shouted Pop.

They both put their weight on the end of the timber. One end of the slab moved up as nice as you please, and I slid the fence post under it.

After another hour of grunting and groaning, we had the slab resting on four fence posts right at the foot of the ramp leading up to the bed of the truck. Getting out the block and tackle, Pop tied one end of the heavy rope around the slab of stone and fastened the pulleys to the cab of the truck. Then he and I pulled on the rope while Mike pushed on the stone.

I'll bet I was the most surprised kid that ever tried to get a slab of stone out of a quarry. Ever so slowly, the slab moved up the ramp toward the truck.

We had it about halfway up the ramp when disaster hit. Slowly the front end of the truck swung up into the air. There was nothing we could do to stop it. When it finally came to a stop, the front wheels were four feet off the ground. The slab slipped backward and clipped Mike in his good pants. Tore a big hole right out of one knee, and Mike said a cuss word or two before he remembered I was there.

You can't beat Pop, though. He climbed up on the hood of the truck until his weight tipped the front end back down. The tires no sooner hit the ground than he was ordering Mike and me to pass up some rocks. In ten minutes he had the hood of the truck weighted down with about a ton of stone.

Well, we worked for another hour, and believe it or not we finally got that slab up into the truck. When we stood back to look at our work, we discovered something else. The stone was so heavy that the truck springs were squashed flat and the rear fenders were no more than eight inches off the ground When we got in the cab and added our own weight, the truck scraped the ground.

There's something about a job like that that gets into your blood. By that time, both Mike and I were so all-fired mad at that slab of stone that we were *determined* to get it home. We'd had so much trouble already that we'd have carried it home on our shoulders.

As it turned out, Mike and I walked and Pop drove the truck. Every once in a while the bottom of the truck would scrape loud enough to make Mike shudder. Pop didn't dare go any faster than we could walk. At midnight, four miles is a mighty long way to hike, especially when you have to watch out for bumps that might hang up a pickup truck loaded with stone. We made it, though.

The worst part, that time of night, was unloading the slab at the house. Pop backed right up to the front porch. Under the slab were the fence posts, and somehow we managed to roll the stone across the porch and through the front door into the living room. Pop said he wanted it out of sight of prying eyes.

It was two-thirty in the morning by the time we finished. Betts had made some coffee for Mike and Pop, and a cup of hot chocolate for me. It tasted mighty good that time of night, as I sat on the slab of stone.

Pop and I were dog tired and headed for bed. Just before I turned out the light I heard Betts and Mike speaking low and soft to each other.

"Look at my good pants," said Mike. "Ruined."

There was a long, long pause. I'm not as young as some people think. I knew they were kissing each other.

Finally Mike said softly, "That makes the whole evening worthwhile."

Now that's a lot of mush.

How Pop Carved Atlas

With the whole weekend ahead of him, Pop flew at that slab of stone like a wildcat after a field mouse. He used not only the sculpting tools but also a bunch of old chisels from the tool shed. The living room began to look like Main Street the day they tore it up with air hammers. Every once in a while Betts would wink at me then bring me a broom to sweep up the mess. She knew he'd tire of sculpting before long, but he'd never be satisfied until he'd tried his hand at making a full-sized stone statue.

We were in for a surprise. The more the chips flew, the more that stone began to look like something—not much at first, but it sort of grew on you. Pop said he was going to make a full-size statue of Atlas—you know, the ancient god that held up the world.

Day by day, that slab looked more like a man. At first there was just a ring around the middle, a ring that later became Atlas's waist. Then his chest took shape, and I swear you could even see the ribs in it, with the shoulder blades coming down in just the right direction.

The legs and feet were next. Working with a mighty fine chisel, Pop even put toenails on Atlas. The arms were the hardest part; he had trouble shaping them just right so they looked like they were holding up something. Last of all came the head. That's when Pop had his worst luck.

The nose flew off. Just flew right off and landed in the magazine rack. Pop tried gluing it back on, but it didn't look right, so he tossed it back in the magazine rack. In the end that stone was transformed into the figure of a strong man with his arms raised as though he were holding up something. Pop planned to add the world later, from another piece of stone.

And don't let me give you the idea that the statue was a perfect job except for the nose. It wasn't. There were holes here and there where the chisel had slipped, and one side of the head looked like it had been bashed in by a hammer. As a matter of fact, it *had* been bashed in by a hammer.

After the nose flew off Pop began muttering as he worked, and I could tell that he was unhappy with Atlas. On Saturday night he asked Betts and Mike and me to take a look.

"What do you think?" he asked.

I didn't know what to say. The thing looked goofy, standing in the middle of the floor.

"Looks like a man," I said.

56

"Not bad," said Mike. "A lot better than I thought you could do."

"Mighty fine," said Betts. But she said it in a low voice.

For two minutes nobody said anything else. Atlas stood there, glaring at us with his bashed-in head. He wouldn't win any prizes, and I think Pop knew it.

Finally he dropped the hammer he held in his hand, and let out a long trembly sigh. "I guess it isn't so good."

That's one thing I admire about Pop. He faces reality. There's no nonsense about him. I always say it's better to face reality than try to fool yourself. You might want to remember that.

Pop walked out across the front porch, his shoulders hunched over as though he was almighty tired. He stooped and picked up a fence post. "Come on," he said in a low voice, "help me take Atlas back to the quarry."

We all felt sorry for him. "If you're sure you don't want it," Mike said, "couldn't we just dump it out in the woodlot?"

Pop shook his head. "Nope. That old piece of stone belongs to the quarry, doesn't it?"

He'd never worried about that before, but Mike and I were on his side now. We picked up some fence posts, too, and went to work.

Atlas weighed a lot less now than when he had come out of the quarry, but it still took us two and a half hours to get him back there. We managed to tumble

58

him off the truck at just about the same spot we'd picked up the slab of stone.

All that time, Pop hadn't said a word. When we drove out of the quarry, he didn't even look back.

Mike and I did, though. I shined the flashlight back alongside the cab. The light wasn't too steady as we jounced along, and Atlas's shadow sort of jumped, as though he was alive.

Made me feel like I'd thrown out an old friend.

...8

How Willy Peters Went Back into Business

When I make a slingshot, I like to use rubber cut from an old inner tube. Some kids buy special rubber tubing, but not me. I ran out of rubber strips, so Monday morning I hiked downtown to see if I could pick up a new old inner tube from Mr. Schwartz, who runs the garage.

Just as I walked up to the garage, the Aldrich twins came riding by on their bikes, yelling like crazy.

"Hey!" I shouted. "What's up?"

When they saw who was heying them they skidded to a stop. One of them—I can't tell them apart—said, "Did you hear the big news?"

"What news?"

"They found a putrified man out in the quarry."

"What do you mean, 'putrified man'?"

"You know. Putrified. Turned to stone."

"You mean *petrified*," I said, "like petrified trees that fell to the ground a thousand years ago and turned to stone."

"Yeah. That's right. Petrified. There's scads of people out there already, looking at the petrified man."

All at once I knew what had happened. I started to laugh.

"What's the matter, don't you believe us?"

I was about to tell them about Pop and his sculpting when it suddenly occurred to me that there'd be a lot more excitement around town if I kept my mouth shut.

"You're crazy," I said. "There aren't any petrified men around here."

They started arguing, and pretty soon they insisted I come along with them to see the petrified man. One of them rode me out to the quarry on the bar of his bike. We didn't make very good time, because news about the petrified man already was spreading around town and a good many cars were headed in that direction.

We jounced down the back road that led to the quarry, and rounded a bend. There we bumped right into the biggest crowd I'd seen since the lion tamed Pop. People were milling all over the place, trying to get a peek at the petrified man.

I squirmed in through the crowd, snuck between a man's legs, and ended up in the front row. There at my feet was Atlas. People were rubbing their hands over him, talking about his petrified skin and "Look! No eyeballs." I had an *awful* time trying not to laugh.

Right up in the front row was Willy Peters. His

62

hands were in his pockets and instead of looking with wonder, like the rest of the crowd, he was gazing down at Atlas with a cold and calculating eye. I knew if there was a penny in Atlas's stone pockets, Willy would manage to get his hands on it.

All day I stayed there, watching the crowds come and go. A good many of the people were picking up stone chips for souvenirs—just like the stone chips that were buried in the concrete all around their houses. In the middle of the morning, a dozen of the men surrounded Atlas and, just as carefully as if he was a dying man, they eased him over onto his side. Somebody put a car cushion under his face so he wouldn't get hurt, and they rolled him onto his stomach.

At noon, during the lunch hour back in Fairfield, the crowd must have doubled in size. That was when I spotted Pop and Mike. There was a smile hidden in Pop's wrinkles, and Mike was pretending to be amazed by the petrified man. They caught my eye. It was just as though they'd spoken the message: Don't say a word, came through to my brain, loud and clear.

By evening somebody had rigged up a portable generator with floodlights. The crowd kept right on looking and feeling Atlas's skin long into the night. Betts had brought me a sandwich, so I hung around until about nine o'clock. Minnie Wumpser was there. I'm telling you, it was a big temptation to tell her that I knew all about Atlas, and that he wasn't a petrified man at all but something Pop had sculpted. I swallowed the temptation, somehow.

63

When I returned home, Betts and Pop and Mike were really laughing it up.

"Best joke I've ever played," declared Pop. "Glad I thought it up."

You see how Pop is? Already he was taking credit for something he hadn't even planned.

The next day a truck with a derrick showed up at the quarry. Half a dozen men rolled Atlas onto a heavy canvas sling and swung him up into the truck. The crowd began to grumble. Already the people of Fairfield considered that petrified man their property.

Willy Peters was there. When someone tried to stop the truck, Willy spoke right up.

"This outstanding specimen of a petrified man," he said, "legally belongs to the Ames brothers who own the quarry. He's their property, according to every law in the state." He cleared his throat, as though he was going to make a special announcement. "I've made an arrangement with the Ames boys to exhibit this fine specimen. If you want to look at him anymore, come out on Highway 16."

"How much will it cost, Willy?" shouted somebody in the crowd.

"Not much. Fifty cents a head, twenty-five for kids."

There was a lot of bellyaching at that, but the truck drove off with Atlas. I followed it out to the highway.

Do you know what Willy had done? Already he'd rented Oostermeyer's fruit stand, right along the edge of the highway, and closed up the sides so you couldn't see in. Atlas disappeared into the fruit stand, and it

64

wasn't thirty seconds until Willy appeared at the door with a roll of tickets in his hand. When Pop heard about it, it made him madder than an ugly peacock to think that Willy was making a fortune off his talent.

Naturally there was a big story in the Fairfield paper about the petrified man, and the *State Capitol Register* ran a picture of Willy patting Atlas on the stomach.

Out along the highway appeared some new signs:

SEE THE ONLY PETRIFIED MAN IN THE U.S.!
WILLY PETERS ENTERPRISES

And

SEE THE STONE-AGE MAN THAT TURNED TO STONE!
WILLY PETERS ENTERPRISES

Within twenty-four hours, people were flocking in from all directions paying fifty cents a head (twenty-five for kids) for a peek at Atlas. Pop's statue rested on a gold-painted table, and there was a big batch of candles at Atlas's head and another at his feet.

Even though I didn't have twenty-five cents, I couldn't stay away from Atlas. All the next morning I sat across the road watching people disappear into one end of the fruit stand and walk out the other.

At one o'clock in the afternoon, a man with a bristly beard appeared at the fruit stand and shook hands with Willy Peters. I walked across the road.

". . . head of the Department of Anthropology at the

65

state university," the man was saying through his beard. "Heard about your find and drove over to check it out."

I could tell Willy didn't want him around, but when the professor threatened to announce that the petrified man was a fraud, Willy finally let him through the door. *Correction*: Willy let him through *after* getting his fifty cents.

Willy cleared out the crowd and closed the door behind him so he and the professor could be in there alone with Atlas.

When the professor came out, he didn't say a word, just drove off in his car. The evening paper, though, carried an article:

PETRIFIED MAN ISN'T REAL, SAYS PROFESSOR

FAIRFIELD, Aug. 22. Professor Tyler Jackson, noted anthropologist of the State University, today announced that the "petrified man" of Fairfield is not genuine.

After a detailed examination of the "body," Prof. Jackson stated that it had been carved from stone.

"It definitely is not a man," he said, "although it may well be a statue from some past civilization that inhabited this area. I intend to notify the art section of the University's archaeology department. Perhaps Dr. Fleming can shed some light on the mystery."

There must be something about tourists that make them *want* to part with their money because they still

66

flocked to see Atlas. Tourists from two dozen different states didn't care whether he was a *real* man or a statue, as long as he was something they could pay to see. Willy had a bigger day than he'd ever had before.

Next morning, though, trouble showed up again. The man from the art department of the university drove over to examine Atlas.

For a long time, maybe two hours, he stayed in the fruit stand. By the time he came out, a big crowd had gathered, including Wyn Cox, who is a reporter for the Fairfield paper. Wyn stopped the art professor at the door.

"Can you give me a statement for the local paper, professor?"

"Be glad to," said the man, biting out each word. "The statue was carved by a sculptor about 500 B.C. It definitely shows the Inca influence, although until now there has been no trace of an Inca civilization this far north. The sculptor was a remarkable man. Using primitive tools, he created a masterpiece that could put most of our modern sculptors to shame."

Pop was standing right beside me. I thought he would bust. His chest swelled up, he got red in the face, and one leg started moving up and down. Even Pop can't hold his breath forever, and it finally came out in a long, long sigh. He was proud enough to turn inside out.

"You say that statue is a masterpiece?" he piped up in his high voice.

"Definitely," said the man.

All of a sudden Pop started waving his hands and yelling.

"I did it!" he shouted. "I carved that statue on the living-room floor a few days ago. It's *my* masterpiece! *I'm one of the greatest sculptors in the world!*"

Most of the people, I'm sure, thought Pop was off his rocker. They gathered around, trying to calm him. He finally called on Betts and Mike to back up his story.

Nobody believed them either, until Pop had an inspiration. "Follow me!" he shouted. "I'll *prove* that statue is mine!"

He headed across the road toward our place. The whole crowd tagged along. Traffic on Highway 16 was held up for blocks.

Pop took the crowd on a tour. He showed them the pile of stone chips out behind the woodshed, the hammer and chisels he'd used, the scratch marks where we had moved the slab of stone across the floor.

Finally he had the best idea of all. He dug through the magazine rack until he came up with a chunk of Atlas's nose. Trotting back across the road, he matched up the chunk with the hole in Atlas's face. Everybody believed him then, even though Willy Peters kept shouting, "Don't listen to the old fool! He's a fraud!"

The crowd began drifting away. The man from the state university was the first to leave. His face was mighty white, and I noticed his hands trembled as they gripped the steering wheel. The others didn't say

68

SEE THE ONLY
PETRIFIED MAN
IN THE U.S.

WILLY PETERS
ENTERPRISES

much, just shook their heads, climbed in their cars, and drove off.

That left Willy Peters standing alone by the fruit stand. We all went home.

For the rest of the afternoon, nobody said much. Now that Pop had announced to the world that he was a great sculptor, he didn't seem to be getting much pleasure out of it. At the supper table he sat there, grumbling down his wrinkled neck.

Finally he said, "I think I'll go over and say good-bye to Atlas."

Somehow it sounded like just the right thing to do.

Things wound down after that. The paper said the art professor got fired. A week ago a man from New York made a special trip here to see Pop. All the art critics, he said, consider Atlas a fine example of "the primitive influence in modern art" (whatever that means). He offered Pop a wad of money to sculpt a statue of "Liberty and Justice" for the lobby of a skyscraper they're building in New York. Pop turned him down cold. He's through with sculpting.

The next morning I rode into town with Pop in his pickup truck. At one point, the truck sort of drifted off toward the side of the road. I looked up at Pop to see what was the matter. He was driving with one hand, fingering his shirttail with the other. He swerved back onto the road just in time.

Down the road apiece he said, "Pete."

70

"Yeah, Pop." I looked at him. There was a new light in his eyes.

"Pete, how would you like to help me with my new hobby?"

"Sure. What's your new hobby, Pop?"

"I sent for a book awhile back, but didn't get to it until just now. Pete, it's the most exciting thing in the world! We're going to learn how to hypnotize people!"

...Part III

Pop Potts, Hypnotist

...9

How Pop Hypnotized Chickens, and How He Tried to Hypnotize Noah Oostermeyer's Pig

Nothing else exists for Pop when he launches himself into a new hobby.

Pop just couldn't put down that book on hypnotism. He'd tried hypnotism as a hobby once before, with zilch results. Now I had the feeling he might be onto something big. He'd rush home after a day's work and gulp down the supper Betts had fixed. Sinking his skinny little body into the easy chair, he'd open the hypnotism book. All evening he'd sit there, eyes feverish, trying to learn how to hypnotize people.

I could see it coming—the day he was going to try to hypnotize someone. When that day arrived he came slamming into the house shouting, "Betts, you'll have to postpone supper for a while!"

"But Pop," she said, "I fixed turnip stew for you tonight."

That stopped him for a minute. I was washing up at

75

the kitchen sink, and I could see the battle going on inside. Which was more important—turnip stew or hypnotism?

"The stew will just have to wait," he said finally. "I've got some practicing to do out by the hen house."

That shows how a hobby can take over a person's soul. You might want to remember that.

Betts smiled at me and turned down the fire under the stew. I set out a plate and some silverware for Mike, who'd be home soon. I knew we'd be involved with Pop for a while.

Betts and I have talked about Pop lots of times. She says we shouldn't try to change Pop, because he's an exciting person to live with. I sure can agree with her there. Living with Pop is like living on the edge of a cliff. That's why we were excited, too, when we followed him out to the hen house.

"What's on your mind, Pop?" I asked.

"I'm going to do some hypnotizing."

"Hypnotizing?" said Betts. "Then why did you come out here to the hen house?

Pop snorted as though anybody would know the answer to that. "Why, anybody would know the answer to that," he said. "Just like it says in the hypnotism book, you start out slow and easy. You start out on birds and animals."

"You mean you're planning on hypnotizing some chickens?" I asked.

"Yep," said Pop, unlatching the hen house.

76

"I've hypnotized chickens lots of times," I said, bragging. But I meant it.

I don't know whether you've ever hypnotized a chicken or not, but it's easy as anything. First you've got to catch the chicken. Then you tuck its head under one wing. Holding it tight in both hands, you sort of swool it around in a circle, a dozen times or so. When you set down the chicken it'll stay perfectly still for just about as long as you want.

I'm not kidding, it really works. If you don't believe me, try it. You unhypnotize a chicken by poking its head out from under its wing so it can see again.

"I know you've hypnotized chickens before," said Pop, "but the book says you need a lot of practice. Now quit dawdling and help me catch some of these varmints."

Well, we hypnotized chickens for an hour or so. Betts and I would catch them, and Pop would swool them around and put them to sleep. Finally we had twenty-five or thirty chickens standing around still as statues without any heads.

I couldn't see that we were accomplishing anything except hypnotizing twenty-five or thirty chickens, so I finally said so.

"I'm going to tell you something, Pete," he said, "and I want you to remember it all your life. Whenever you take up anything, you've got to master it a step at a time. I suppose you think it's fun for me to stand around here hypnotizing chickens. Well, let me tell you it's pretty tiresome. But everything in life takes practice. You might want to remember that, Pete. It makes a fine thought for the day."

He whirled another chicken around in a circle and set it on the ground.

"Now for the second step," he announced. "Pete, drag that old board over here and lay it on the ground."

I hauled over the board and plopped it in front of him.

"Now I'm going to show you how to hypnotize a chicken with method number two."

Pop pulled a piece of white chalk from his pocket. "Pete, grab that big chicken over there."

It wasn't easy. I finally caught it in the corner of the fence.

"Now," said Pop, "shake it good, and then hold its beak down against the board."

I'm telling you, I was mighty surprised at what happened. I shook the chicken like a paint mixer. It squawked bloody murder and tried to get away, but I had a good hold. I put its beak down on the board.

Along the board, right in front of the chicken's eyes, Pop drew a nice white chalk line. The chicken got stiff as a stone, and its eyes glazed over.

"Let loose," said Pop in a whisper.

When I took my hands away, the chicken just stayed there looking at the chalk line. Maybe you won't believe me, but method number two works. Try using chalk the next time you want to hypnotize a chicken.

We went on practicing for another half hour. When

78

Pop finally figured he had practiced enough, we stepped back to look over our work. There was a line of chickens straight down the board like soldiers on parade, all gazing at the chalk line. Not a feather moved. It was quite a sight.

"What do you think of that?" said Pop.

"Pretty good," I said.

I think Betts was getting interested now, too. "What's method number three?" she asked.

Pop didn't answer for a minute. He stepped up to the board and pushed over one chicken with his foot. The whole line of chickens toppled like a row of dominoes. They went squawking off in all directions.

"Now," announced Pop, "we're going to hypnotize a pig."

"That's pretty hard to do," I said, "mainly because we don't have a pig."

"I thought of that," Pop replied. "You'll have to run across the road to Oostermeyer's. Go along the back fence so nobody will see you. Skin in behind the barn and catch one of the young pigs. Bring it over here right away."

"I can't do that, Pop. That would be stealing. And you know what they do to pig stealers in this county." I didn't know what they did to pig stealers in this county, but it sounded good.

"It's not stealing, Pete. We're just borrowing that pig for an hour. It's an experiment to advance the science of hypnotism."

We argued, but Pop finally won as usual. A few min-

79

utes later I found myself sneaking along behind Oostermeyer's barn. When I climbed into the pigpen I made sure I was out of sight of the house.

Did you ever try to catch a pig? I always say a pig is as hard to catch as a shark in a farm pond. Those Oostermeyer pigs scattered in every direction, shaking the ground like a buffalo stampede. I finally got hold of one of the young ones, held it by both hind legs, flung myself over the fence and ran for home.

"What held you up?" asked Pop, standing there with the flashlight he'd fetched from the kitchen shelf. When he's hobbying he has no patience. "Betts, you hold the varmint's hind quarters, and Pete, you grab the front legs and head. Hold him just as still as you can."

Anybody knows you can't hold a pig still. All you can do is keep him from jumping. Betts and I did our best.

Pop walked around in front of the pig. "Hold up his head so he can see me," he said.

I held up the pig's head.

Pop turned on the flashlight and started swinging it in a little circle right in front of the pig's eyes. At the same time he made cooing sounds deep in his throat.

The flashlight scared the pig out of its wits. We would have lost it if Betts hadn't kept hold of its hind legs.

For fifteen minutes Pop tried to hypnotize the pig with the flashlight and the little sounds in his throat. The more he tried, the more scared the pig got. Even

81

Pop finally lost patience. He said if a chalk line would work on a chicken, maybe it would work on a pig too. We tried that a couple of times, but it didn't work, either.

"No sense in trying to hypnotize *that* pig," said Pop in disgust. "It's plain to see there's something wrong with it. It's a mighty sick pig, and if I were Noah Oostermeyer I'd get rid of it right away, before it sickens the others in the litter. Pete, you take that pig away from here right now. I don't want it on my property. It's diseased."

Oostermeyer didn't catch me when I returned the pig, so I can't be accused of pig stealing in this county, unless Noah Oostermeyer reads this book. Stealing the pig was a terrific chance to take.

Like I always say, people treat you exactly the same way you treat them. If you're nice to them, they'll be nice to you. If you try to skin them, they'll try to skin you. What I'm trying to say is that Noah Oostermeyer probably would have loaned us a pig if we'd just told him we wanted to hypnotize it.

When I got back home the turnip stew was on the table. Even then it was hard to get Pop to eat. He was rereading chapter 3 of the hypnotism book.

...10

How Pop Hypnotized Me, and How Mrs. Smithers Threatened to Put Me in the School for Wayward Boys

The night after I borrowed the pig I was dead tired. All day I'd been helping grub the suckers out of the corn patch down the road, and I was too tired even to finish a book I'd been reading. I just about fell asleep on the sofa.

Pop was sitting in the easy chair, poring over the hypnotism book as usual. When you see Pop read you're watching a real stage show. He moves his lips to form the words, and whispers some of them out of the corner of his mouth. Every once in a while, when something is particularly exciting, he'll suck air through the gap in his front teeth. It makes a whistling sound like a jet plane roaring through the living room.

I was lying there on the sofa watching him read that night. He was sucking air faster and faster. Finally I got up, yawned, and stretched. It was just at that moment

83

that I saw the idea hit him in the face like he'd run into a two-by-four.

"Pete," he said, leaning forward, "there's nothing to this hypnotism. Just because we happened to get our hands on a sick pig doesn't mean I can't hypnotize a human being. I could do it like *that*"—he slapped his leg and the dust rolled out of his overalls. "Why, with the secrets revealed in this book I can have anybody completely in my power." He looked at me. There was a long pause. "Even you, Pete."

"Oh no you don't, Pop. When you wanted to be a detective, I let you chase me halfway across the county. But I'll be darned if I'll let you try *hypnotizing* me."

"It won't take long." Pop stood up as though it were settled.

Well, to make a short story even shorter, Pop wouldn't let me go to bed until he'd tried hypnotizing me. He bustled around the room turning off all the lights except the one standing right behind the easy chair. He made me sit in the chair with a pillow under my neck, and my feet propped up on a stool. He wrapped the light at my feet with a sheet of newspaper, then made a hole in the paper so that only one bright beam of light came through. It was sort of spooky.

"Pete, that business of looking the hypnotizer in the eye is old-fashioned. We're going to do it the modern way. Just look at that spot of light, relax, and listen while I read to you out of this book."

I gazed at the light.

"You're completely relaxed," Pop said. "Every mus-

84

cle in your body is tired. You're calm and peaceful. More than anything in the world, you want to sleep."

Pop read a lot more stuff like that. His voice kept droning at me. "You want to sleep . . . sleep . . . sleep. Your eyes are getting tired. Your eyes are getting heavier . . . heavier . . . heavier. . . . You can't keep your eyes open. You can't stay awake. You're going to sleep . . . to sleep . . . to sleep. . . ."

I know it sounds fishy, but that's the last thing I heard. I was so all-fired tired I *did* go to sleep. The next thing I knew, Pop was yelling in my ear.

"Pete! Pete! Wake up!"

I opened my eyes and yawned.

"By jabbers, it works, Pete!" Pop went dancing across the room. "I'll be a dog-eared pig if it doesn't work! I can hypnotize people. I put you to sleep!"

When I tried to explain that I was so tired I just naturally fell asleep, he wouldn't listen.

"Don't you believe it, Pete. I put you to sleep like it says in the book."

And you know, right then I didn't know for sure whether I'd fallen asleep or he really had hypnotized me.

He was all for going ahead with the hypnotism lesson, but I just plain refused and hauled off to bed. I woke up once in the middle of the night and could hear him tossing and turning. I knew he was too excited to sleep.

The next day I didn't have anything in particular to do, and neither did Joey Gootz. Betts and Mike were

85

working, and Pop was patching a leak in Pilchard's barn roof.

Joey and I drifted up the creek, trying to find some crawdads. We didn't find many, and about the middle of the morning Joey picked up a wad of mud and heaved it at me. Caught me smack on the Adam's apple and made me madder than a billygoat. I hit him with a mudball behind the right ear. Pretty soon we were having so much fun with the mudball war that I forgot about being mad at him for hitting me in the Adam's apple.

Dodging from tree to tree on each side of the creek, we fought our way back toward the house. I didn't stand much of a chance, because Joey is the champion mudball thrower of Fairfield. We've never actually had a city mudball-throwing contest, but I *know* he'd win if we ever had one.

Back by the hen house, Joey picked up some overripe eggs and started heaving them. One caught me right on the belt buckle. Have you ever been hit on the belt buckle by a rotten egg? The only smell I can think of that's any worse is the home of an old civet cat.

We washed off at the rain barrel, but the smell didn't come out and there was still a lot of mud on our clothes. We drifted into the house and sat down to rest.

Sitting in the easy chair, Joey reached out and picked up Pop's hypnotism book.

"What's this?"

I explained about Pop trying to hypnotize people.

"Hypnotize me," he said.

86

I waved my hands toward his eyes, and he pretended to be hypnotized. He leaped to his feet, arms straight at his sides, and went stiff as a board, with his eyes bulging out. I can't think of anybody that can get as stiff as Joey. He can make himself as straight and strong as an oak beam. I gave him a shove back into the chair, and he sort of toppled over.

"Try it for real," he said.

I looked at him a little doubtfully. "Do you really want to be hypnotized?"

"Sure."

I pulled down all the shades in the living room and turned on the table lamp. I had Joey relax in the easy chair with a cushion under his neck and his feet on the footstool. Then I blotted out the light except for one little beam, just as Pop had done. Joey was grinning at me past his crooked nose. It got hit by a steam shovel when he was five. I finally found the place in the book.

"You are relaxed. . . . Your eyes are heavy . . . heavy . . . heavy. . . . You are going to sleep . . . to sleep . . . to sleep."

Joey closed his eyes, but there was a big grin across his face, and I knew he was just pretending.

At that moment I heard a step on the front porch. There was a rustling noise at the door, and I waited for somebody to knock. When there wasn't any more noise, I knew somebody was standing at the screen door trying to see into the room. I went over to see who it was.

If I could have my pick of anybody else in the

world, I would have picked anybody else. It was Mrs. Smithers.

I *know* there's some good in everybody, but it's mighty hard for me to see it in Mrs. Smithers. She's a big woman who always wears too many clothes. She's the *nosiest* person I ever met. She has to know every little thing about everybody in town. Then she goes and blabs it to everybody else. Maybe she's lonesome because Mr. Smithers is so busy at the bank, but why does she have to stick her nose into everybody else's business?

Betts said that whenever the women of the church have a meeting, Mrs. Smithers has to run it. When there's a school election, she always says who will be the candidates. When the state college glee club comes to sing each Thanksgiving, she makes all the arrangements, including who will stay at who's house. She's just a plain old busybody.

But worst of all: it was Mrs. Smithers's rose garden that Joey and I had knocked over with the leaky water tower. She's never said anything about it because she couldn't *prove* who'd done it, but she knew we'd loaded that cannon just as sure as though she'd watched us do it.

"Hello, Mrs. Smithers," I said through the screen door. "Nobody's home."

"You mean nobody's home *with you*," she said, sniffing. Mrs. Smithers sniffs when she talks.

She pushed the screen door right against my face and edged into the room. The easy chair squeaked.

88

"Who's that?" she said sharply.

"Just Joey. Joey Gootz."

"What are you boys doing in here with all the shades down?"

I didn't know exactly what to say. "I was hypnotizing him," I blurted.

"*Hypnotizing* him!" she repeated. She sniffed again, and this time I guess she sniffed the rotten eggs. She stuck her nose in the air and looked down at us, first one then the other. Our clothes were all mucky.

"What a filthy pair of boys. I've never seen anyone dirtier. And you *smell*, too."

"It's rotten eggs."

"No self-respecting family would live this way. Good heavens! Boys as filthy as pigs, with all the shades pulled down, and nobody knows what deviltry you're planning."

"We aren't planning any deviltry. Just hypnotizing."

"What kind of nonsense is that? What you and your sister need is some discipline—from an adult. It's plain to see that you haven't had any discipline since your parents died, Peter Potts."

That made me mad. Pop, Mike, Betts, and I live a perfectly normal life. Besides, what business was it of hers?

"I think you'd better go now, Mrs. Smithers."

"Are you ordering me about, young man? Disrespect for your elders. I won't go until I find out exactly what mischief you two boys are up to."

"I told you. We were hypnotizing."

89

"Show me this instant."

Well, I couldn't see any other way to get rid of her. Even though I didn't want to, I picked up the book and began to read to Joey, who was still sitting in the easy chair.

"You are sleepy. . . . Your eyes are getting heavier . . . heavier . . . heavier. . . . You can't keep them open. . . . You are going to sleep . . . to sleep . . . to sleep."

My voice droned on for two or three minutes.

I didn't see the idea hit Joey, but I'm telling you, I *felt* it. I could almost read Joey's mind. Still talking, I glanced up. His eyes were closing. I began to make up the words myself.

"You are asleep . . . asleep . . . asleep."

His eyes were completely closed now. I could feel Mrs. Smithers there beside me in the darkened room.

"You will stay asleep, but you will open your eyes," I said.

Joey's eyes snapped open like they were on barn-door hinges, and his eyeballs bulged out, staring straight ahead toward the far wall.

"You will stand up . . . stand up . . . stand up."

Slowly and stiffly, as though in a trance, Joey got up from the chair.

"You are a board. . . . You are stiff as a board."

Joey gave a tremendous jerk and just plain froze. You wouldn't think he was the same person, he was that stiff. Beside me, Mrs. Smithers let out a gasp, then a loud sniff.

90

I moved the footstool. "Take one step forward," I said.

Joey goose-stepped forward, his knees stiff. I walked around behind him and put my hands on the back of his head.

"You will fall backward . . . backward . . . backward."

He tipped himself back into my hands, and I pivoted him down like a tent pole, until the back of his neck was resting on the front edge of the chair. Then I went around in front, kicked the stool into place, and put his heels on it.

I'm telling you, he looked as straight and stiff as a railroad tie. His head was barely on the chair, and his feet were barely on the footstool. Mostly there was nothing but air under him. I looked up at Mrs. Smithers. She had sort of a glazed look in her eye, as though she was hypnotized, too.

Stepping over to Joey, I sat down on his stomach and crossed my legs. Joey can stay stiff all right, but I kept most of my weight on one leg instead of on him.

"Sit down, Mrs. Smithers," I said, patting Joey on the chest, "and tell me your troubles."

She let out a shriek and ran for the door. When she was halfway through she turned around and began shouting.

"Peter Potts, you are not fit to associate with the other children in this town. Just look at you. All covered with mud and rotten eggs." She started to sniff and then thought better of it. "You live in all this filth, with nobody to watch over you. It's no wonder you've turned out this way."

I was getting pretty mad. I stood up and started toward her.

"There's not a child in this town—or an adult either—who's safe with you around," she raved on, "and I aim to do something about it. Oh, yes! Just wait until I tell the judge about *this*. I guarantee that within a month you'll be in the School for Wayward Boys. And that's just where you belong. *The reform school!*"

"You wouldn't talk that way," I said, "if Pop was around."

"Don't double up your fists and threaten me, young man!" I hadn't even noticed they were doubled up. "Just wait until I tell the judge that you threatened me!"

"Don't worry, Mrs. Smithers," I said, trying to keep my temper. "I wouldn't threaten you. I'd just—" I paused a moment. "I'd just *hypnotize* you."

She let out a holler and ran across the porch and out toward the road.

I walked back in. Joey was still stiff, but when he heard the door slam he dropped to the floor. We looked at each other and started laughing.

It didn't take me long to get over that laughing spell. The thought of reform school was like a cold hand on my shoulder. The reason I was so worried was because

93

the judge was Mrs. Smithers's sister-in-law's brother-in-law, and I figured that I already had two strikes against me.

"Yeah," I said to Joey, "she can put me in the reform school all right."

And I'm telling you, I'd be there right now if it weren't for Pop and his hypnotism.

...11

How Pop Hypnotized Joey Gootz and Me

When Pop came home from Pilchard's, Joey and I were going to tell him about Mrs. Smithers's visit, but he was so excited about hypnotism we didn't have a chance.

The first thing he did when he walked in the house was to throw his cap on the stuffed crow (he can do it from clear across the room) and grab the hypnotism book.

"Now I want you kids to help me," he said. "I'm ready for the next step—hypnotizing two or more subjects at the same time." Pop was always talking about people as subjects, because that's what the book called them.

He made us sit on the sofa, side by side, with our feet propped in front of us. His hands were shaking so he could hardly hold the book. I think he was in a hurry to try the experiment before Betts came home and talked him out of it.

"You kids relax," he said. "Both of you listen to what I say, and don't pay any attention to each other. I'm not only going to put you to sleep but I'm going to *make you do my bidding*."

I didn't know exactly what that meant, but I figured we'd humor him for a while. It might soften him up a little and keep him solidly on our side when Mrs. Smithers started sending me to the reform school. There are problem spots in life when you need as many people as you can get in your corner. That's a good thought for the day.

Just before Pop began droning away at us, I glanced at Joey out of the corner of my eye, and he gave me a big wink. I figured he was up to something, but I didn't know exactly what.

"You're completely relaxed," said Pop, pointing to the beam of light from the lamp. "You're looking at the light and relaxing. Your eyes feel heavy. . . ."

He went through the whole routine, just the same as before. Joey's right hand was beside mine on the sofa, and just as Pop said "You're going to sleep, to sleep, to sleep," Joey nudged me. I knew then what he was going to do, so I closed my eyes.

"You are asleep," said Pop. "You are asleep and hear nothing but my voice." There was a long pause, as though Pop was trying to screw up his nerve to try something new. Then he said, "You can hear

96

nothing but my voice. If you understand, nod your head."

I nodded my head with my eyes closed. Beside me I could feel a little movement of Joey's body, so I knew he must be nodding, too.

"You are completely in my power," said Pop. "You are in my power, and anything I tell you to do, you *will* do. Now open your eyes."

My lids snapped up, and I sat there staring at the ceiling.

Out of the corner of my eye I could see Pop jumping up and down, doing a little jig. "I did it!" he mumbled to himself. "I did it! They're both hypnotized, and they're doing exactly what I say!"

I guess he had to check the book, because pretty near a minute passed before anything else happened. I tried to keep my eyes from blinking.

"When I say the word *now*, you will stand up. You will get to your feet when I say the word." There was a pause. Then, in a loud voice, "Now!"

Joey and I stood up. I could feel Joey standing there stiff as a poker, the way he can do, so I tried to make my body just as stiff as I could.

There was a whistling sound as Pop sucked air through his front teeth. I don't think I've ever seen him so excited, even the day Prince arrived at the railroad station. "I've got 'em!" Pop muttered. "I've got 'em in my power!"

Then, aloud, he said, "When I give the order, you

97

will start walking. You will continue to walk until I tell you to stop. Now, *walk*!"

Joey and I started across the room, side by side. Joey kicked over a can of fish worms we'd left on the floor, but neither of us paid any attention.

"Stop walking," said Pop.

We stopped.

He put us through a whole routine. First he had us bend over and touch the floor ten times. Then we stood perfectly still with flowerpots on our heads. Pop nearly died laughing. He thought he had us hypnotized, all right.

After a while he got out a pencil and paper and had us write "I'm a babboon," three times. On his paper Joey wrote "I'm a babboon three times," as though he'd misunderstood. That set Pop to laughing again. I think he had us write the sentence to prove he'd hypnotized us, once he woke us up.

Finally he had us stand in the middle of the room, staring straight ahead. "Now I want you to flap your arms and crow like roosters. You are roosters. You are roosters."

Joey started flapping his arms and going "Cockadoodledoo, I'm a rooster. Cockadoodledooooo!" I did the same thing, feeling pretty dumb. I was getting tired of fooling around this way.

That's when Joey headed for the door. He kept flapping his arms and saying "Cockadoodledoooo!" Just as he passed me he gave a big wink. I roostered across

98

the room after him because I knew something was up.

"Stop!" called Pop. "You're not roosters anymore."

Joey and I kept right on moving. When Joey got to the door he acted as though it wasn't even there. He just brushed right on through it, with me bringing up the rear.

"Stop!" shouted Pop. "Stop! Wake up!" I could hear him jumping up and down behind us. We didn't even pause.

Across the porch and down the steps we crowed. As we moved out across the yard Pop was shouting, "I got 'em hypnotized and now I can't wake 'em up! What'll I do? Oh, what'll I do?"

Joey had a real inspiration this time. He strutted across the yard, crowing at the top of his voice and waving his arms like they were wings. I'll bet Joey can do a better rooster imitation than anybody in the whole state. I found myself imitating Joey instead of a rooster.

Pop was dancing along behind us shouting "Wake up! Wake up!"

Do you know what Joey did? He did what any rooster would do: he headed straight for the hen house. I was right at his heels. When we got there he pushed open the gate, crowing like crazy. Those hens must have thought they were being invaded by an army of lonely roosters. It was just like an explosion: chickens flew all over the place. I turned just in time to see three of them hit Pop in the face.

99

Joey choked on a "doodledo" and turned red. The door slammed shut behind us, with Pop on the outside.

Joey and I looked at each other and started laughing. We laughed so hard the tears came.

But the last laugh was on us. We hadn't been in the hen house thirty seconds when the door flew open and we were practically drowned with cold water. Pop had run out, turned on the hose, and shot water into the hen house to wake us out of our hypnotic trance.

I got a mouthful of water and stumbled blindly toward the door. Wet chickens were dropping all around. Finally I staggered out, grabbed the nozzle from Pop, and pointed it at the ground.

Pop turned off the water. "You kids all right?" he asked anxiously.

I spit out some water. "Yeah." Joey just nodded his head.

Pop's chest started swelling. Then he was dancing on one foot.

"Do you kids know what happened? I hypnotized you. I had you completely within my power. I made you do everything I said. When I told you you were roosters, you headed straight for the hen house. By jabbers, it works! I can hypnotize anybody. I can get anybody completely within my power!"

He was so excited we didn't have the heart to tell him what had really happened.

As a matter of fact, it was sort of exciting for us too, and I forgot to tell Pop about Mrs. Smithers's visit until after supper. When I told him, he got madder than a rooster himself. Said if she came poking her nose around the house again, he'd poke it right back. And he told me not to worry about reform school.

I noticed, though, that both he and Betts seemed mighty worried when they were talking about it.

...12

How Mr. Gootz and Pop Got in an Argument over the Price of Land for a New Playground

Joey Gootz's dad is a pretty nice guy, even if he and Pop don't get along very well. Mr. Gootz plays ball with us, and he's always organizing stuff for kids, from Easter-egg hunts for the little ones to kick-the-can games for those of us who are almost grown up. He's one of the few adults I know that really seems to have *fun* with kids.

And kids aren't the only ones who like Mr. Gootz. Most every grown-up in town thinks he's tops, too. For as long as I can remember he's been on the town council. Whenever anybody is in trouble, they go to him. And he does a lot of good things nobody knows about except Mrs. Gootz and Joey and myself. Joey tells me lots of times. Mr. Gootz does things like taking six pairs of shoes to Mrs. Lumpkin, who is a widow who has a flock of kids, every few months. The

103

shoes, not the kids. And dropping off turkeys to certain people at Christmas time.

What I like about Mr. Gootz is that he doesn't make a big show of being good to other people. The more he can hide it, the better he likes it. I always say if you're going to be bad, do it with a bang, but if you're going to be good do it just as quietly as possible. That's a double thought for today.

Pop is the only one in town that doesn't get along with Mr. Gootz, and that's because of an argument they had a couple of years ago. The town council was remodeling its rooms and asked for bids from the three carpenters in town. Mr. Gootz was in charge of the arrangements. Pop put in his bid, but the Allen brothers were lower. Mr. Gootz gave them the contract instead of Pop. It really made Pop mad.

"You'd think he'd give me the contract because Joey is a good friend of yours," said Pop.

I didn't see it that way. I don't want anybody—even Pop—trying to make money off my friendship.

Maybe you don't think this has anything to do with Pop and his hypnotism, but it does. Mr. Gootz was pretty important to Pop's hypnotism.

Like I said earlier, we live on the edge of Fairfield. Pop's land snuggles right up against the city limits. That's what made it so valuable.

At a town council meeting a few months ago, Mr. Gootz said it was a shame the kids in town didn't have a decent playground. There are playgrounds at the two schools, but not much else. Fairfield is growing—the population was up fifty-nine at the last census—and Mr. Gootz said now was the time to build a nice playground before we had too many kids and not enough land.

Well, that set off an argument. Most of the council agreed with Mr. Gootz, particularly when he pointed out that there was enough money lying idle in the town treasury to build the playground.

Mrs. Smithers isn't on the town council, but she always attends the meetings and makes speeches. This time she got to her feet and said there was no sense in wasting money on kids—that they'd get in trouble even if they had a playground. That started the fight. I guess it was one of the hottest meetings the council ever had.

In spite of Mrs. Smithers, the council voted to spend eighty-five hundred dollars on a playground, complete with all the equipment. And the mayor gave Mr. Gootz the job of finding the land, buying it, and building the playground.

You'd think there would be a lot of good places for a playground in a town like Fairfield, but there aren't. About all that's left in the way of land is a few vacant lots, none of them big enough.

That's what brought Mr. Gootz over to see Pop one night. Betts had just finished the dishes. I was putting a new bobber on my fishing pole, and Pop was studying his hypnotism book, when there was a knock at the door.

Pop opened the door, impatient because he had

been taken away from his hypnotism book. There stood Mr. Gootz and Joey. I guess Joey came along to see me.

"Evening, Cadwallader," said Mr. Gootz. Cadwallader is Pop's real name, but nobody calls him that except Mr. Gootz, who uses first names with everybody.

"Well?" said Pop, blocking the doorway. He was still mad about the contract to remodel the council room.

"Can I come in?"

Pop stood there for a minute. Then he moved back from the door. "I always believe in being hospitable to everybody, *even those who aren't hospitable to me.* Come in and state your business."

Mr. Gootz and Joey came in and sat down. Mr. Gootz took out his pipe, filled and lighted it. I think it made Pop mad that he took so much time.

"Evening, Mr. Gootz," said Betts, sticking her head around the kitchen door.

"Evening, Betts. My you're looking pretty these days. How's Mike?"

Betts blushed.

"Gootz," said Pop, "you didn't come over here to tell my granddaughter how pretty she is."

"Nope. I want to talk a little business with you, Cadwallader."

Mr. Gootz told Pop all about the plans for the new playground. The more he talked, the more excited it made Joey and me. He even talked about a swimming pool sometime in the future.

106

"Now, Cadwallader," said Mr. Gootz, leaning forward in his chair, "I've looked at all the land around town, and there isn't much available. As a matter of fact, the best piece of land for the playground is that two-acre tract of yours right next to Linden Street."

"That land isn't even inside the city limits," said Pop.

"No, but we can move the city limits if we can get the land."

I figured Pop would sell the two acres right away. Since Grandma died, he hasn't done any farming to speak of. More than once he'd told Betts and me that he thought he'd sell some of his land and invest the money.

It was a big surprise when Pop said, "That land isn't for sale, Gootz."

Mr. Gootz went on talking in that low voice of his, sucking on his pipe. He explained what a wonderful thing that playground would be for the kids in town. He pointed out that the land was ideal. Part of it was cleared, and there were some big oak trees on the rest of it.

"Furthermore," he said, "that land is idle now. It's not doing you a bit of good, and you're paying taxes on it."

"I'm aiming to farm it again someday," said Pop. I know he didn't believe it. He thought for a long minute. "How much were you figuring to pay for it?"

"I reckon a fair price for that much land on the edge of town is five thousand dollars."

Pop snorted. "Why, it's worth twice that much."

I saw then what he was trying to do. He wanted to sell all right, but he was trying to boost the price out of spite.

"Idle land costs money," said Mr. Gootz.

"Well, I wouldn't say that. It gives me a deal of pleasure just to own that land."

"Quite a piece from the house here, isn't it?"

"Not exactly. Once I start farming again, it will make a nice tractor ride over there of a morning."

"The fence around it is mighty loose."

"Might need a little fixing in spots, but it's the stoutest fence on my land."

They wrangled that way for half an hour, Mr. Gootz pointing out that Pop didn't need the land, and Pop declaring it was the best two acres in the state.

Pop finally came down to $8200, and Mr. Gootz finally came up to $6200, but that was the closest they got. Mr. Gootz pointed out that $6200 was all the city could afford if there was going to be enough money left over to change the land into a playground and put the proper equipment on it.

They both grew more stubborn by the minute. By the time Mr. Gootz left, Pop was huffy. He stood in the open door and shouted, "I think I'll plant both those acres in alfalfa next year. And you keep off my land!"

Betts and I tried to calm him down. We both wanted him to sell, because we thought the playground would be a good thing. And we both knew he *wanted* to sell,

108

because he'd told us so in the past. But he wouldn't budge.

"If Gootz wants that land," he said, "he's going to pay a pretty price for it."

He was still sputtering when he went off to bed.

"There goes the playground," I said to Betts.

"I'm afraid so, Pete. Sometimes Pop can be as stubborn as a dead mule."

...13

How Joey Gootz and I Hypnotized Pop

After supper the next evening Joey drifted over. We sat around within earshot of Pop, complaining that there wouldn't be any playground in town. I guess the idea was bothering Pop some, too, because he didn't suggest trying any more hypnotism experiments.

Finally he said to Joey, "When does your father report to the town council?"

"Thursday," said Joey. That was two days away.

"What's he going to say?"

"Already written the report," said Joey. He never says much, so every word counts. "Carries it in his pocket. You won't sell the land. No other land worth a hoot. No playground." Joey shrugged.

Pop turned back to the hypnotism book. He has a big conscience, but he also has a big stubborn streak. I knew he was fighting himself inside.

Joey and I went out along the road to look for owls. We didn't see any, so Joey went on home.

111

When I walked back into the house, Pop was still reading the hypnotism book. All of a sudden he jumped out of the chair, as excited as a dentist at the sight of a bad tooth. "Pete," he said, "I've got it! Here's the solution to the whole problem. Tell Joey to have his father drop over here tomorrow night. Maybe we can still talk business."

"What's come over you, Pop? First you lean one way about that playground, then the other."

"Look here," he said, pointing to a paragraph in the book. "Read what this says."

I read out of the book: "The subject can be made to fulfill the minutest legal formalities and will do so with a calm, serene, and natural manner. When he is awakened he will recall nothing of what has happened."

"What does it mean, Pop?" I asked.

"It means I can hypnotize someone and make him sign any papers I want."

"So what?"

"So I'm going to get Gootz over here, hypnotize him, and make him sign an agreement to buy that land *at my price.*"

I wiggled that thought through my brain.

"Do you think that's fair, Pop?"

"I don't know about that. But it wasn't exactly fair for him to give the Allen brothers that job at the town hall, either."

It seemed mighty shady to me, but I knew when Pop's mind was set it was like concrete.

112

"Get me a pen and paper, Pete."

He sat down at the table. While I watched over his shoulder, he wrote: "The undersigned parties agree that two acres of Cadwallader Potts's land will be purchased by the town of Fairfield for a price of $8200. Signed: _____" Then he left space for Mr. Gootz's signature and his own.

He made two copies, one for himself and one for Mr. Gootz, "just to make it legal." When he was through he put them in a white envelope and tucked it in his overall pocket.

"Now," he said, "when Gootz comes over tomorrow night I'll hypnotize him and have him sign those papers. I'll put one copy in his pocket instead of the report that's already there. Oh, I'll get my price out of him all right." He was practically dancing with glee.

Me, I didn't know what to do. I was sure that Pop wanted to sell that land, and I was sure that he wanted the playground. But he was so cussed stubborn that he wouldn't let himself make the deal. And now he was going to do it in an underhanded way.

The next morning Joey and I had a long powwow about the problem. I told him Pop's plan.

Finally we came up with a way to use Pop's plan to skin Pop himself. Before we could do anything, though, we had to get that envelope out of Pop's overall pocket.

By late afternoon we still hadn't solved *that* problem. When Pop came home he was so excited about skinning Mr. Gootz that he was close to exhaustion.

113

He took off his shoes and sank down in the easy chair, eyes flashing.

"Tonight, by jabbers!" he said. "Tonight's the big night. Nobody except you boys knows that I'm a first-class hypnotist, that I can get anybody in my power. Tonight's the night I get back at Gootz for that slimy trick he played on me." He let out a sigh of exhaustion.

It was then that the idea struck me like a post pounder.

"Pop," I said softly, "do you reckon I could hypnotize anybody?"

"I don't know. It's pretty hard. Why don't you try it on Joey while I relax? If you have any trouble, I'll help you out."

"Why don't I try it on *you*? If you're going to be a hypnotist you ought to find out how it feels to *be* hypnotized."

He nuzzled the thought. "You know, Pete, you might be right. If I'm going to hypnotize everybody into voting for me for governor, I'd better learn the business inside out."

You see how Pop is? Already he had every voter in the state hypnotized.

I pulled down the shades and fixed the light. The room was almost dark, and Pop's feet were propped up on the stool.

"I don't reckon you'll succeed in hypnotizing me," he said, "but just in case, promise me one thing. No nonsense. No roosters or anything like that."

"I promise."

114

Well, I started saying the words into his ear, slow and easy, repeating everything I had learned. I made my voice as soft as possible, and droned on and on. When I came to the part about his eyes getting heavy, heavy, heavy, I got the biggest surprise I've had since the hornets crawled out from under the radiator. No kidding. Pop's eyes closed, and he started breathing from deep inside his skinny chest.

You may not believe I hypnotized him. Myself, I still don't know what to think. Maybe he was exhausted from a day's hard work and the excitement of the evening ahead. Maybe he just naturally fell into a sound sleep. Maybe I hypnotized him. I don't know.

But he *did* go to sleep, snoring away with a thunder that shook the house. I glanced at Joey. His crooked nose was wiggling, the way it always does when he's excited.

"You did it," he whispered. "You hypnotized him!"

"I don't know whether I did or not," I whispered back, "but he's asleep, and that's what we want. Be careful."

I reached out and touched the pocket of Pop's overalls. He didn't stir. Moving my hand as sly as a weasel in a hen house, I managed to get my fingers into his pocket. Finally I snagged the corner of the envelope between my fingers and hauled it out. Pop kept right on sleeping.

Joey handed me another envelope, one we had already prepared. I pushed it into Pop's pocket and looked at Joey. We'd done it.

115

"While he's hypnotized," suggested Joey, "let's make him think he's a hound dog chasing a coon. That ought to be quite a sight."

I was tempted but didn't try it. I'd promised Pop I wouldn't fool around. I always say you shouldn't make a promise unless you intend to keep it. That's an inspiring thought for the day.

Even now, though, when I think of Pop lying asleep in that chair, I wish that I had told him to wiggle his big toe, or scratch his nose, or do *something* so I'd know for sure whether I had hypnotized him.

Instead I reached out and shook him by the shoulders. I had trouble waking him up, and when his eyes opened they looked like he'd been drugged.

"What happened?" he said.

"I hypnotized you."

He snorted and rubbed his eyes. "That's a lot of nonsense, Pete. I was so tired I just plain fell asleep." There was a little doubt in his voice, though. He pulled himself up out of the chair. "Come on. Let's peel the potatoes. I want an early supper tonight. I have an evening of hard hypnotizing ahead of me."

...14

How Pop Thought He Skinned Joey's Father

Promptly at seven o'clock there was a knock at the door. For the past half hour Pop had been fussing around, getting the room ready.

Earlier, when Betts had come home from work, I'd managed to get her down to the hen house out of earshot of Pop. I'd told her our plan, and she agreed it was the right thing to do if we could get away with it.

Pop was a lot friendlier to Mr. Gootz that night.

"I've been thinking about that piece of land," he said. "Might be we could get together on it after all. Sit down a spell. A little later in the evening, we'll talk about it."

Hauling out his pipe, Mr. Gootz said, "Mighty nice of you to reconsider, Cadwallader. You know my hands are tied by the town council. I can only repeat the final offer I made the other night."

Pop waved his hand as though it was unimportant. "We'll talk about it later." He picked up the hypnotism

119

book and waved it around, as though by accident, while he tried to find other things to talk about. "How's business?"

"Fine. Fine."

That afternoon, Joey had told his dad our plan, so Mr. Gootz was all primed. He took Pop's bait like a channel catfish. "Say, Cadwallader, what's that book you have there? Looks like it might be interesting."

"It's all about hypnotism," said Pop. "Did you ever see anybody hypnotized, Asa?" It was the first time he'd called Mr. Gootz by his first name since the trouble over the contract.

"Nope. Can't say that I have. Must be fascinating to see it done."

Pop couldn't wait to give the line a jerk. "I can hypnotize people."

Mr. Gootz's eyebrows shot up. "Cadwallader, you're kidding. You can't really hypnotize anybody."

"Sure can. I'm probably the best hypnotist in the state. Want to try an experiment?"

"Somebody might get hurt." The catfish was playing with the hook.

"Gooseberries! Nobody will get hurt. I've hypnotized hundreds of people." Pop knew this wasn't true, but he was too excited to bother about a little exaggeration.

"Wel-l-l-l." There was a doubtful tone in Mr. Gootz's voice.

"Oh, come on. I'll tell you what I'll do. I'll hypnotize you, so you'll know how it feels."

120

"You can't really hypnotize me, Cadwallader."

"I'll bet you a jug of apple cider that I can. You just sit right over here in the easy chair, facing the lamp."

Pop practically forced Mr. Gootz into the chair, and he turned out all the lamps except one. He propped up Mr. Gootz's feet and told him to relax.

"I feel like a fool," said Mr. Gootz.

A smile spread across Pop's face. "Never mind about that. Just listen to my voice."

Pop got down close to his ear. "You are relaxed all over. Every muscle in your body is relaxed. Your eyes are heavy . . . heavy . . . heavy. . . . You are going to sleep. Your eyes are heavy and you're going to sleep . . . to sleep . . . to sleep. . . . Close your eyes and go to sleep."

His voice was soft as a kitten's fur. You know, *I* felt a little sleepy, listening to it. After about three minutes Mr. Gootz let out a long sigh and closed his eyes.

Pop looked at Betts and me. His eyes shone like a cat's in that half-dark room. "I've done it!" he said. "I've got him in my power!"

He looked down at Mr. Gootz. "You are sound asleep. You will stay asleep even when I tell you to open your eyes. You will stay asleep. Now—open your eyes."

Mr. Gootz's eyes flickered open. They stared at the ceiling. When he didn't bat them even once, I got flibberty inside. I began to wonder if he *really was hypnotized.*

"Move your right hand up and down," said Pop.

121

Mr. Gootz's hand waggled on the arm of the chair.

"Now stand up." Pop's voice was high-pitched and trembly.

Letting out a long sigh, Mr. Gootz stood up.

"Come over here to the table."

Joey's dad looked like he was walking in his sleep, staring straight ahead.

Pop reached into his overall pocket and pulled out the envelope. He brought out the two sheets of paper. In the dim light it was difficult to see what was written on them. Pop placed them face up on the table.

"Take this pen in your right hand." Of a sudden he looked over at Joey. "He *is* right-handed, isn't he?" Joey nodded.

Mr. Gootz took the pen.

"Now sign your name at the bottom of these papers."

Mr. Gootz signed.

Pop started to fold up the papers. "You'd better sign them yourself, to make it legal," I whispered.

He grabbed the pen and scrawled his name on both sheets. He sealed one of the papers in the envelope and handed the other to me. "Keep it where it will be safe," he whispered.

Mr. Gootz was standing there straight as the tail of a peeved skunk. Reaching carefully into Mr. Gootz's coat pocket, Pop substituted his envelope for the one he found there. "Just wait till he reads his report to the town council," he said with a giggle.

"Sit down in the chair again," he ordered. Then, "Wake up!"

122

Nothing happened.

"Wake up!" said Pop again.

Still nothing happened.

Pop looked over at me, frowning. "Hope I don't have to shoot the hose on him," he whispered.

"Wake up!" he said real loud, and clapped his hands.

Mr. Gootz jumped out of the chair. He looked around the room kind of sheepish, and when I turned on the lights his eyes blinked as though he had just awakened from a long night's sleep.

"What happened?" he asked.

"I hypnotized you. You've been asleep."

Mr. Gootz looked mighty dazed. "Well, I'll be swoggled, Cadwallader. You mean you really hypnotized me?"

"Yep."

Shaking his head as though he couldn't believe it, Mr. Gootz repeated, "Well, I'll be swoggled."

They sat and talked about hypnotism for fifteen minutes. Finally Mr. Gootz said, "Well, that was mighty interesting. Mighty interesting indeed, but it's not getting any work done. Now about the price of that land, Cadwallader—"

"No need to discuss that," Pop broke in. "I'm sticking to my price."

Mr. Gootz pretended to get real mad. They ranted at each other for five minutes. Finally Mr. Gootz flung himself out the door, shaking his fist over the "waste of time."

Pop waited until he was sure Mr. Gootz was out

123

of earshot. Then, laughing and slapping his leg, he shouted, "I did it! I did it! I skinned Gootz with my hypnotism. Pete, let me see my copy of that paper he signed."

I had a sinking feeling. "Oh, I'll take care of it, Pop. You might lose it at work tomorrow. I'll put it in the sugar bowl, where it'll be safe."

"You do that, Pete. By jabbers, we really have Gootz where we want him now. Pete, you and I and Betts are going to that town council meeting tomorrow night. I can hardly wait to see Gootz's face when he opens that envelope and reads aloud what's inside. And Pete—if he doesn't read it, I'll take my copy right up and slap it on the council table. Nobody can skin Cadwallader Potts and get away with it!"

...15

How Pop Got Skinned in Front of Everybody at the Town Council Meeting, but Was Happy about It

It was the biggest council meeting I can remember since they voted to build a steel water tank. Word had gotten around town about the playground, and a good many parents were there to see that their council voted for it. Most of the grown-ups were gabbing about how good it would be to have a fine playground for the kids.

All except Mrs. Smithers. As usual, she was sitting in the front row, practically on the platform where the mayor and the council sat. From the way she was sniffing and then squeezing the corners of her mouth, I knew she'd do everything she could to stop the playground.

Just once she looked at me, but that one look was enough to freeze ten gallons of boiling water. Her eyes

125

seemed to say, It won't be long until you're in reform school.

Mayor Jeff Bean called the meeting to order. There was some other business to take care of, but the council got rid of it in a hurry.

Then the mayor said, "And now we come to the report on the playground. You have the floor, Mr. Gootz."

"Just a minute!" shouted Mrs. Smithers. "I have something to say about this." She got to her feet and turned halfway around, so both the audience and the council could see her.

"Playground? It's a waste of money. My tax money and yours. We don't need a playground in this town. What we need is more discipline by the parents. What we need is parents who'll look after their kids—not an expensive playground with a lot of expensive equipment on it.

"Give the children of this town a playground, and what will they want next? A swimming pool! Give them a swimming pool and they'll want a dance hall. There'll be no end to their demands.

"No, we don't need a playground. A child's place is at home, not on public property. His place is at home, where his parents can look after him—that is, *if there's anyone home to do the job!*"

She swung her head around and looked straight at me. A few years ago I had a butterfly collection. I stuck the butterflies to a board with two pins. Looking into Mrs. Smithers's eyes, I felt like one of those butterflies.

126

"There are *certain* children in this town," she went on, "who are just naturally bad. I am thinking of one in particular. He has no adult supervision whatever. Just the other day I found him and one of his playmates in scandalous trouble. Let me tell you, I intend to bring this matter before the judge tomorrow. No, we don't need a playground. What we need is some real parental discipline." Mrs. Smithers sat down.

A lot of people in the crowd started talking at once. I was scared because of what she'd said, and I looked up at Pop. He patted my shoulder to buck me up, but I could see the worry lines around his mouth. I'm a goner, I thought.

The mayor banged his hammer on the table. "Thank you for expressing your opinion, Mrs. Smithers," he said. "It's always good to have heard what you think." He didn't say it was good to hear it, but good to *have heard* it.

"Your honor," said Mr. Gootz, getting to his feet. "I'd like to make my report now, as it may serve as a basis for further discussion."

"Go ahead, Councilman Gootz."

Mr. Gootz reached in his pocket and pulled out the white envelope. "I have here a signed statement, which I would like to read."

Pop nudged me. His toes were twitching. "He's going to get skinned in front of this whole crowd," he whispered.

"As you know," Mr. Gootz went on, "we had hoped to buy a satisfactory piece of land for a playground for

127

a maximum of sixty-two hundred dollars, the remainder of the money to go for equipment. I would like to read you this signed statement."

Pop was quivering.

Mr. Gootz took out the paper and read: "The undersigned agree that two acres of Cadwallader Potts's land will be purchased by the town of Fairfield for a price of $6200. Signed, Asa Gootz. Witnessed, Cadwallader Potts."

There was a moment of stunned silence, then every parent in the room looked at Pop and started shouting and clapping.

Pop was so flustered he hardly knew what he was doing. "Give me my copy of that paper," he whispered.

Reaching in my pocket, I took out the piece of paper and handed it to him. He read it.

"I've been skinned," he whispered. "Somehow I've been skinned."

Everybody was standing and clapping and waving at Pop. His mouth twitched a little, and slowly he began to smile. Then he was laughing and waving back at the people.

Mr. Gootz grabbed the mayor's hammer and banged for order. "Attention, please!" he shouted. "Attention! Attention! I suggest we name the town's new playground 'Cadwallader Potts Playground' in honor of the man who made it possible!"

Well, I thought the roof would blow off. Everybody cheered. Somebody shoved Pop to his feet, and he

128

bowed in all directions, then clasped his hands over his head like a boxer who's just won a big fight.

After ten minutes of whoopdeedoo, things settled down. I saw Mrs. Smithers stick her nose into the air and stomp out the door. Pop saw it, too. He looked down at me and grinned.

"She won't dare do anything now, Pete. After all, I'm one of the town's leading citizens. They even named a playground after me. She won't dare say I'm not fit to raise a decent boy and fine girl."

I'm telling you, that's the biggest load I've ever unloaded off my mind. No reform school! Wow!

I knew deep down inside that I hadn't *really* done anything bad. Oh, I've tossed a few rotten apples in my time, shot a hole in a water tower, and bashed in the front end of a hearse, but the water tower and hearse were strictly accidents. Like I always say, kids get in trouble by accident. That's a good thought for the day.

Pop and I rode home in the pickup truck. He sat there in silence. I knew he was trying to figure out what had gone wrong with his hypnotism, and how he'd signed the note without realizing it. He kept glancing at me. I think he suspected I'd helped skin him, but he couldn't figure out how I'd done it.

After a while he sort of shrugged and gave out a long sigh.

Then, just as he turned into our drive, he let out a yip. I looked at him. His eyes were shining in the dim light.

130

"Pete, I've got a new hobby. Best one yet. Want to help?"

"Sure. What're we going to do?"

"Believe it or not, Pete, we're going to build us a two-man helicopter, and then fly it to Walla Walla, Washington."

Pop stopped the truck and got out. I sat there thinking about what he'd said. It sounded exciting. I climbed out and slammed the door. "Why Walla Walla, Pop?"

"I always liked the name. Walla Walla. Kind of rolls off your tongue. Yep, that's where we're flying, Pete. Walla Walla."

At any moment, life can take a new and exciting turn. You might want to remember that.

There's not much left to tell. Although one other thing *did* happen that would drastically change my life. Betts asked me to walk up to Pretty Place with her. That's what we in our family have always called it, because that's what it is. It's a mile up the creek from our house. There's a little grassy spot right on the edge of a tiny waterfall, all shaded by some big willow trees.

Betts had been mysterious about our trip up there, and if I'd known what she had in mind I probably wouldn't have gone. We sat on a log beside the creek and watched the water dance across the rocks. There was kind of a strained silence. It didn't seem like Pretty Place at all.

Finally Betts cleared her throat and said abruptly,

131

"I'm pregnant, Pete. I'm going to have a baby. After Mike I wanted you to be the first to know."

I thought about that for a minute and then was surprised at my reaction. For the first time since Grandma died, tears rolled down my cheeks. When I could talk, I said, "That means you and I won't be a family anymore."

"Oh, no, Pete! We'll still be a family! It's just that the baby will be a part of our family, too."

I glanced up at her and instantly thought of my mother. That's a funny thing. I was so young when my parents died that I can't remember them at all. But sometimes when I suddenly look up at Betts, I think of my mother.

I tried to stop the tears but couldn't. All I could think of was that some *thing*—some *body* who wasn't even born yet—would come between Betts and me.

I guess I sobbed a little with the tears running down my face. Then, right in the middle of a sob, I hiccuped.

That hiccup helped me grow up. At least a little bit. Kids do that, you know. Something new will happen to them, or they'll think a brand-new and deep thought about their parents or God or something else important, and they'll give a spurt toward growing up. My spurt theory explains why kids suddenly get tearful or mopey or go off on some planet of their own. They're spurting. You might want to remember that. I spurted because I suddenly realized that any baby born to Betts would be a *special* baby. *Especially to me.*

132

How could I object to that? The tears stopped rolling, and I looked over at Betts. I licked the salt from my upper lip and grinned.

"I'll show him our Secret Place out in Kellogg's woods," I said. "It belongs to Mike and me, but we'll let *him* know about it, too."

"Already it's a boy?" She spoke it as a question.

"Got to be," I said. "You're the only girl I'll permit in this family."

She put her arms around me. "I'm so happy, Pete. And at the same time a little bit scared. We don't have much money for the doctor and the hospital and all the diapers he'll need. Oops! I guess you're right. It *will* be a boy."

"I'll save some money for you," I said. "Maybe I can get a job out at the canning factory." You can see how much I'd spurted in just two minutes.

She hugged me, and we sat there in silence. I was being thankful for her and Pop and Mike—and the new baby. I was thinking how my life seemed to be just right for me. Believe me, that's unusual. *Almost never* does a kid think about being thankful. Ask any kid and he'll tell you I'm right. Most of the time, if we do anything, we complain. But once a year or so (and it *never* happens on Thanksgiving), it occurs to almost every kid that he's pretty lucky. He thinks about it for a while. Pretty near a whole minute.

134

About the Author

Clifford B. Hicks began writing professionally as a reporter for the Des Moines *Register and Tribune* when he was still in high school. He subsequently attended Northwestern University and continued his writing career while working as an editor with a scientific and mechanical trade magazine in Chicago. Mr. Hicks currently lives in Brevard, North Carolina, where he is an editor with *Popular Mechanics*.